Praise for Deborah Adams and her Jesus Creek mystery series

"Compassionate, chilling, and compelling."
—GILLIAN ROBERTS

"Deborah Adams brings the rustic wit and wisdom of Lake Wobegon to the plains of middle Tennessee."
—SHARYN MCCRUMB

"Thoroughly enjoyable ... A mystery novelist to be reckoned with."
—*Nashville Banner*

"Adams captures both the intricacy and style of a well-crafted mystery, along with the comic elements of a truly Gothic Southern novel. In the process, she transcends both."
—STEVEN WOMACK

"Adams's books perfectly capture the rhythms of life in a small town, where everyone sees it as a God-given right to know everybody else's business."
—*The Baltimore Sun*

"Adams has a fluid, soft, and delightful writing style.... A terrific writer. My personal library contains all the 'All the' novels to date, and I'm leaving plenty of room for more to come."
—*The Nashville Tennessean*

By Deborah Adams
Published by Ballantine Books:

(In chronological order)

ALL THE DEADLY BELOVED

Deborah Adams

BALLANTINE BOOKS • NEW YORK

Copyright © 1995 by Deborah Adams

All rights reserved under International and Pan-American Copyright Conventions. Published in the United States by Ballantine Books, a division of Random House, Inc., New York, and simultaneously in Canada by Random House of Canada Limited, Toronto.

http://www.randomhouse.com

ISBN 0-345-39222-1

Printed in Canada

First Ballantine Books Edition: November 1995

10 9 8 7 6 5 4 3

Dedicated, with love and gratitude,
to Jim and Justine

THANKS, GUYS!

Q: How many mystery fans does it take to write a book?
A: One to type, and all these others to provide information and support.

Donald Adams, the love of my life.
Richard Bryant, New Johnsonville police officer.
Don and Jacque Dumas, eternal newlyweds.
Maddox and Maddox, brilliant attorneys.
Jean Newsome, unflappable friend.
Sharyn McCrumb, Mistress of Wit and Whimsey.
Detective Linda Mayo, toughest lady in town.
Ken and Jean Smith, long-suffering parents.
Richard and Debbie Wagoner, spiritual providers.
Kelly Wilhite, woman of many talents.
The Friday Night in the Whimsey Suite Gang:
  Edith Brown, Gerri Lawrence, Taylor McCafferty, Jeff Marks, Margaret Maron, Jean Swanson, Terry West. (This will teach *Megan* not to go to bed so early, won't it?)
Belated thanks to *Ariel McCrumb* for allowing me to use her name in *All the Hungry Mothers.*

Cast of Characters

Lamar Alexander, Howard Baker, and *Al Gore:* future U.S. presidents (Tennessee's hope springs eternal)

Al and Bill: police dispatchers; still struggling with the age-old question *Is it nine-one-one or nine-eleven?*

Sheriff Barlow: Angela County's second-finest law-enforcement officer

James and Anne Barrow: a couple guilty of most forms of psychological abuse

Benny and Chester: mainstays of Jesus Creek society

Amanda Brewer: Dr. Gentry's nurse and an incurable idealist

Delia Cannon: local activist and budding wise-woman

Scott Carter: obnoxious teen with a dark future

Eloise: small-business owner, femme fatale, and good old girl

Cathie Emory: Licensed Practical Nurse at Jesus Creek Nursing Home

Dr. Finster: resident who drives in from Nashville to attend Jesus Creek patients, perhaps because he graduated so far below the other aspiring physicians in his class

Diane Forsythe: charge nurse at the nursing home, unfortunate enough to be stuck on evening shift

Reb Gassler: Jesus Creek police chief and the last of the politically incorrect, nonvulnerable, antisensitive males

Patrice Gentry: an angel—a dead one by the time this story begins

Steven Gentry: devoted physician and grieving husband of the late Patrice

Genny: Dr. Gentry's receptionist

Ivy Harper: another LPN (we seem to have a surplus of those)

Wayne Holland: the man who makes Kay Martin's life bearable

German Hunt: assistant police chief and groom-to-be

Dave and Martha Johnson: elderly couple, working within the light of God to provide spiritual support for the young people of Jesus Creek

D. D. Maddox: the only lawyer in Jesus Creek and therefore doing quite well for himself

Kay Martin: rookie police officer

Henry Mooten: a political hopeful

Frank Pate: Henry's campaign manager

Ned Richardson: resident of Jesus Creek Nursing Home

Pam Satterfield: the bride-to-be; a no-nonsense woman who will have no trouble training German

Roger Shelton: Delia's significant other; a Yankee who isn't even embarrassed about it

Teresa Simmons: a woman playing a dangerous game

Virginia Steele: resident of Jesus Creek Nursing Home; former teacher, which probably accounts for her disoriented state

Mr. and Mrs. Veatch: robbery victims

Frank and Jane Weldon: good neighbors, in spite of what you may have heard from Anne Barrow

Constance Winter: a woman doggedly upholding the traditions of her ancestors, all of whom were crazy

CHAPTER

1

In the sight of God

DID YOU EVER MEET PATRICE GENTRY? Well, it's too late now. We found her dead this morning. Just after my shift ended, somebody called it in.

I'm taking nights now, since German's trying to get his wedding planned. I told him that ought to take about thirty minutes, but he's really buying into this nonsense. I thought the bride was supposed to handle all the details. German goes on about cakes and color schemes and little net bags full of dyed rice until sometimes I think I'll just shoot him and be done with it. Some people would thank me, you know.

And Kay's working evening shift, which she suggested herself—so don't give me any grief about *her* love life suffering. I don't much like her being out alone after dark. She says she's okay with it, but I don't see how she can be.

Anyway, German had just relieved me and I'd gone over to Eloise's for breakfast. Eloise sends her love, by the way, and says for you to come home soon.

Two bites into my sausage and gravy, wouldn't

you know, and the dispatcher calls for me to get out to the nursing home in a hurry. This was Bill, who's only been there for a year. He wasn't around when dead bodies were turning up in every backyard in town, so this one caught him off guard. Tell you the truth, it shocked me, too. After two relatively peaceful years, I was hoping maybe the crime wave in these parts was over for good.

It's looking real nice out Highway 70 right now. April may be my favorite month. By that time the trees have turned green again, and the weather's warm enough so you don't have to wear full winter gear to wash your car. And on that hillside out past town—you know the one—the daffodils and purple phlox are blooming like crazy. I wish you'd been there to see it.

By the time I got to the nursing home, the parking lot was full of women, every damned one of 'em talking at once. Probably the first time in my entire law-enforcement career I'd actually had a secure crime scene, though, because nobody wanted to get too close to the car. You'd think nurses would be used to dead people, wouldn't you? Not this bunch. They'd huddled up together by the outside door, whining and bawling like lost calves.

"Mrs. Gentry had worked the evening shift," German said. He was reading from his notes as we walked around the car, trying to avoid an extended look at the body. "She got off around eleven P.M. and walked out here to the parking lot alone. Way back here, with the trees growing all around—" He shook his head. "Good place for somebody to hide. Could have come at her out of the dark."

And you know how that lot's tucked in the back
of the building, with just one security light at the
far end. About once a week somebody gets a car
window smashed or tires slashed. These women
ought to know better than to walk out to their cars
alone.

Her body had been sitting there all night long,
until one of the day-shift nurses arrived and happened to park right next to Patrice's car and saw
the problem. Somebody'd taken a shot through the
windshield and blew the lady's head half off. Probably just as well I didn't get to eat more of that
sausage. I'd have been greener in the face than
German was.

The front window of Mrs. Gentry's T-bird was
shattered all to hell. Inside, Patrice was sprawled
out in the driver's seat. I circled the car and looked
in from all sides. Blood had splattered over the
headliner and across the dash, dribbling right on
down to the seat before it dried. If you couldn't see
where her face had been, you might have thought
she'd dozed off and would wake up any minute if a
noise disturbed her. I guess she might have fallen
over except for the seat belt holding her up. So
much for driver safety.

I could see that the ignition key was turned on. It
looked to me like she'd started the car before she
was shot and the engine had just kept running until it ran out of gas. Her nurse's cap was on the seat
beside her, and her white uniform sort of blended
in with the white interior, almost like a carful of
snow. Little red drops had splattered on the hat's

green stripes. Made for a gruesome Christmas decoration.

It was like somebody'd scraped my spine with the edge of a knife. You'd think anybody who'd been to war wouldn't fret over one dead body, but there's a big difference. In a war, you know the bodies will be there, and you wear a shield around yourself that keeps the blood and gore and indecency of it all at a distance. It's got nothing to do with you personally.

But coming on a scene like that one was enough to make me want to break down and cry. They don't make the kind of shield that protects you from ugliness in the real world. Another month and I'd be rid of the title *coroner*. I'd be more than tickled to hand it over to somebody else, somebody with a medical degree and a thicker skin.

Anyway, this nurse who found the body was still standing there screaming when the rest of the day shift turned up for work and called us. All the commotion had brought the night shift outside, too, so we had our hands full trying to get the story straight. Finally German singled out the charge nurse from the midnight shift and brought her over to me.

"Reb," he says, "I think you'd better talk to Diane. She's the only one with her wits about her."

Diane Forsythe is about twenty-two, twenty-three, somewhere in there. She's got that farmgirl look. You know: coppery hair, a few freckles, no makeup, just naturally appealing. Looks like the kind of person you'd want taking care of you when you're sick. And she was holding together like a professional, in spite of having worked all night. She was the one who thought to send the night-shift aides inside to hold down the fort. Seems they'd every one stormed out to the parking lot, leaving the patients to fend for themselves.

"Patrice is the evening-shift charge nurse," she told me. By this time she'd pulled off her little hat and was holding it in one hand, with a cigarette in the other, and her coat draped over her arm. It's this crazy spring weather—freezing cold at night, when Diane would have been going in to work, but warm as an island breeze by eight A.M. when she would normally have started for home. Her hair was starting to come loose from where she'd pinned it up, but other than that she looked fresh as a new dollar bill. "I took report from her at midnight—"

"Report?" I was taking notes, because it was clear it would take at least the two of us to get the situation sorted out, and German was already going down the line of caterwauling women by the back door.

Diane nodded then explained, remembering I was a civilian of sorts. "At every shift change, we take report. The charge nurse coming on is updated by the charge nurse going off duty. My shift started at eleven P.M. Patrice told me what meds had been given, the status of each resident—anything that I would need to know about them."

"So you're the nurse in charge on the midnight shift. Is that right?"

She nodded again, a real crisp head movement that went with her professional manner, but she was sucking on that Salem for dear life. "Last night there'd been nothing unusual for Patrice to report. Our residents don't change much, you know. She'd hung around after her aides had gone on home, to finish some charting she hadn't had time for during the shift. I think it must have been about eleven-thirty when she finally left." Diane glanced over at the car where Patrice's body still waited for someone to collect it.

"Are you absolutely sure," I asked her, "that she was the last one to leave? No one followed her outside? Could someone have been waiting here for her?"

"I'm almost certain she was the last to leave. Whether there was anyone out here in the parking lot, I couldn't say. I walked with her to the door, but only so I could lock it after she'd left. We have to do that because some of the residents will roam at night and we can't take a chance they'll get outside."

I didn't tell her, but it sounded to me like a prison—old folks locked inside a brick building, with tiny little windows most of 'em can't even stand up to look out of.

"And you didn't hear anything? Nothing at all?" I asked her.

"Maybe. I'm not sure, but I think I could have heard the shot. Only at the time I didn't pay attention to it. When I was getting the med cart ready, I remember hearing a crash or boom around. It must have been eleven-thirty or eleven forty-five. Something like that." She looked at me to see if I understood what she was saying, and when I nodded, she went on. "I thought one of the aides had dropped something. But no one came to get me, then I got busy and just didn't think about it again."

You ever wonder why people notice everything except what's useful?

I sent Diane on home and went over to the gaggle of little white-suited geese that German was talking to. By this time he'd settled 'em down enough that we were able to sort out names and addresses. Turns out there's only one nurse each on the evening and midnight shifts, and two on day shift. All the others are aides, who give what they call *patient care.* Bathing and feeding and changing bedclothes. One helpful little nugget made a point of telling me that patient care includes giving enemas when necessary, and removing impactions. Don't ask. You'll be a happier old lady if you don't know what's coming for you.

I stuck German with questioning the aides from both shifts, while I went off to the corner with Ivy Harper and Cathie Emory, the two day-shift nurses. Ivy's the one who first noticed the body, and she was still shaking like a leaf in a windstorm. Took a half hour to get what little information *she* had, and Cathie knew less than that. Not that any of it was likely to help solve the case. If you don't catch the killer standing right there, gun in hand, then the solution gets tricky. They both seemed real fond of Patrice Gentry, though. Told me over and over that she was a wonderful woman who didn't deserve to be hurt.

Then German sent the first batch of aides inside and told them to send the others out so we could get their stories. That didn't take long, because nobody'd seen anything. They talked a lot—nerves, I guess—but mostly about how they couldn't *believe* Patrice was dead.

"She was so sweet to the residents," one of them said, and dabbed at her eyes with a balled-up tissue.

"Did you talk to her last night before she left?" I asked her.

"Not really. I said hello while she was charting, but I was hurrying to get fresh sheets for Miss Virginia. Never fails. The minute I come on duty, that women *wets* the bed and starts pushing that call button. Someday she's going to wear it out."

I asked them to call me if they thought of anything, told them not to worry if I had to come back and ask more questions later, and took my leave of the whole lot.

I hate to think what kind of care those patients got for the rest of the day.

While we waited for the second group to come back out, I met up with German in the middle of the parking lot so he could tell me what he'd learned so far. "The midnight-shift aides," he said, "were all making rounds when Patrice Gentry left last night—checking to make sure the patients were where they were supposed to be, cleaning up the ones who needed it, like that. One of them remembers seeing her at the desk, writing in the patient charts. The others couldn't even swear they'd seen her in the building."

We wandered over to the car and checked the asphalt around it, but there wasn't anything like a bloody footprint or a business card that had been left behind. Backtracking, I made a pass across the lot to the back door of the nursing home. A pile of cigarette butts, Diane Forsythe's brand, told me the smoke police had forced her out into the cold for her moments of pleasure. Probably worried the secondhand smoke will kill some ninety-year-old patient.

When the night-shift aides exited, they told us about finding the body, but couldn't even remember who'd called us. That was the most confused bunch I've ever run into. One of 'em kept sniffling and saying, "Oh, but Patrice was practically an angel." And I kept wanting to say: Yeah, well, now she's really an angel.

By this time, of course, the ambulance had arrived and the EMTs wanted to ask *me* questions. They seemed to feel I was about as useless to them as the nurses had been to me. But one of them knew Patrice. Knew her husband, anyway. Dr. Steve Gentry from down at the Medical Center. He's the one who replaced old Doc Porter a few months ago. So once we got the body and the car taken care of, I had to go tell the man his wife had been murdered.

The EMTs thought Dr. Gentry was probably on duty at the Med Center, so I had to make them promise to circle the block a few times before they brought the body in. I sure didn't want the man to find out about his wife's death like that!

Before I could leave, though, I had to give German a jump start. I tell you: we've got two patrol

cars that can't be counted on to roll downhill, four
cops to cover three shifts seven days a week, three
dispatchers working twelve-hour shifts and alter-
nating weekends, and the city council's bright idea
for reducing debt is to cut my budget. Our illustri-
ous Mayor McCullough is sailing along with that
stupid grin on his face like he knows he's got this
fall's election sewed up, but I'm praying for a candidate who'll whip him so bad, McCullough won't
even stick around long enough to pack. Somebody's
got to pull this town together before it turns to
dust.

Gentry's receptionist referred me to his nurse,
who told me he was at the hospital because it was
his day to work emergency and they'd already had
one. I could have told her it was nothing compared
to the emergency *I'd* just had, but she was a pleasant little thing, so I decided to behave myself. I just
thanked her and left, and drove on over to the Med
Center.

Must have been about nine-fifteen, nine-thirty
when I got there. They told me Dr. Gentry was still
in emergency, so I jogged on back there, trying not
to look like I was bringing bad news. Hospitals are
spooky first thing in the morning. Maybe because
it's unnatural for people to be chirping "And how
are we feeling today?" and bustling around under
fluorescent lights so early, clanging trays and
rolling those wicked-looking IV carts up and down
the hall. And then there's all the coughing and
hacking and moaning.

I caught a nurse coming out of one of the treatment rooms in ER and told her I needed to see Dr.

Gentry right away. I guess they stuck her in ER because she'd failed cheerful training. Maybe they figure emergency patients don't deserve polite care or something.

Anyway she gave me this steely look and said, "The doctor is with a patient. You can wait over there."

"Look," I told her, "this is important. I have to see Dr. Gentry right away."

"We don't interrupt the doctor," she said, and put her hands on her hips (which, by the way, could have shielded an entire battalion). "Now, have a seat or wait for him in his office, but keep your voice down." She huffed off into the treatment room and closed the door firmly behind her, making sure I got the point.

I checked her name tag so I could run her through the computer later. I know where she lives, what she drives, and when her tags expire. And I will be watching. Heather Halstead, LPN, had best not cheat any stop signs around here.

Just to be contrary, I refused to sit where she'd told me. Instead I poked around in the treatment room that was open. What the hell kind of air freshener do they use in these places? Smells like a cross between kerosene and cherry lollipops. Across the hall, in the room where I figured the doctor was working, I could hear a deep voice that must have been his, and a woman's higher-pitched one. What worried me, though, was the kid's crying. You never know what horrible accident a kid may have had. I considered leaving and coming back later just so I wouldn't be there when the door opened.

But I knew the EMTs would be arriving any minute, so I stationed myself in the hall and waited.

About ten minutes later that door opened and the doctor emerged. He was looking back over his shoulder at the little girl he'd been treating. Her forehead had been cleaned with that orange-colored antiseptic and some of it was showing around the edges of the bandages. One of her little eyes had already started to turn dark, too. I couldn't help myself—I watched the mother to see if she looked guilty or scared or what. She picked up the kid and gave her a little kiss on top of the head, and I hoped like hell she was just a good mother relieved that her daughter was okay, not a child abuser relieved she didn't get caught.

Gentry stood there and chatted with them for a few minutes, telling the mother what symptoms to watch for. Then he took the little girl's hand and kissed it. "Beautiful lady," he told her, "it has been an honor to serve you."

The kid couldn't have been more than four, but I swear she batted her eyelashes and smiled like Scarlett O'Hara. And when they were leaving, this kid looks back over her mother's shoulder and blows the doctor a kiss.

About then, Heather Halstead, LPN, heaved herself out into the hall and glared at me. "The police chief wanted to talk to you," she told Gentry, and stormed off without another word.

"Reb Gassler, Doc," I said, and I shook the man's hand. "Can we talk privately?"

He didn't look the least bit worried. "Sure. How

about this treatment room? Or should we go up-
stairs to my office?"

"No, no. This is fine." We went into the room
where he'd just patched up the little girl and I spotted a wastebasket half-full of bloody towels.

Gentry leaned up against the examining table
and stuck his hands in the pockets of his lab coat.
"How can I help you, Chief?" he asked. This guy
could have been Dr. Kildare's nicer brother. Pure
sincerity oozing all over the place.

"I'm afraid I have to deliver bad news," I said,
hoping to ease into it.

Gentry tilted his head, looking truly interested
and just the right amount of concerned. "Does this
involve a patient?" he asked.

"No, sir. It's your wife." I waited a beat to let that
sink in, then went on. "I'm sorry to have to tell you.
She was found dead this morning."

He just kept looking at me, like his mind was on
tape delay and he hadn't heard the words yet. Finally he stood straight up, took a deep breath, and
shivered. You know, the kind of shiver that runs
through you when you say *someone's walking on
my grave*?

"Are you all right, sir?" I started to open the door
and get that bossy nurse to come in again, but he
held up his hand to stop me.

"I'm not sure I understand," he said. His mouth
turned up at the edges, like he thought *maybe* this
was a joke and I'd forgotten to deliver the punch
line.

"She was discovered in her car this morning." I
plunged into the story, hoping I could hand out the

details quickly, before he got over the shock of it. "Someone fired a gun through the windshield. The blast hit her in the face. I'm sorry."

"In her car? Where?"

"In the parking lot, behind the nursing home. We're still investigating, but I'll let you know as soon as we have more information."

Gentry shook his head. "You know, Patrice's car has been vandalized twice in the last two months. I told her she ought to drive my old one. It's such a wreck, a few more dents wouldn't matter."

They usually do babble like that, unless they scream and cry. I wasn't worried, but I didn't want to leave him alone, so I opened the door and looked down the hall for the nurse. Naturally she wasn't there when she was really needed.

"Doctor, the EMTs are bringing your wife's body in about now. Maybe you'd like to get out of here before—"

"Here? They're bringing Patrice here?" He pushed past me and ran out into the hall, over to the double doors where the ambulance unloads. The timing couldn't have been worse, because just then the EMTs pulled the doors open and there was Patrice Gentry's body, covered with a sheet.

I started to grab Gentry's arm, either to hold him back or hold him up, but he took off before I could get to him. He stood there like a sentry at the door between heaven and hell. I still wonder what was going through his mind right then.

The EMTs didn't know whether to wiggle the gurney on through the door or hustle it back out to the ambulance. Before they could make up their minds, Dr. Gentry stepped outside and lifted the sheet. He leaned down and kissed his wife's dead hand, just the way he'd kissed that little girl's. Then he passed out cold.

CHAPTER

2

In the presence of these witnesses

STEVE GENTRY WOKE UP STUNNED. THE
EMTs had hauled him back into the treatment
room where he'd tended to the little girl earlier and
where I'd told him about his wife. By the time they
got him up on the table, he was already starting to
come out of it. Didn't ask "Where am I?" though. I
guess for a doctor, it seems perfectly natural to
wake up in the emergency room.

I was standing in front of the door, right at the
end of Gentry's feet, so he spotted me first. He
raised his head up a little and asked, "Patrice?"

I assumed he was asking if she was really dead,
not mistaking me for her. There wasn't a kind way
to do it, so I just shook my head. He knew what I
meant. I started to move closer to him then, meaning to ask if he had any idea who'd want to kill his
wife, but Heather Halstead had waddled back in
and taken charge.

"Hold it right there," she said to me, and put one
paw on my chest. "You can leave now. Doctor will
talk to you later."

I might have asserted my official authority, but
Gentry had curled up into a ball and started cry-

ing, so it didn't look like I'd get much out of him anyway. I smiled at Heather and said, "Whatever you say, Beautiful." Then I made a quick exit while she was still thinking it over.

Word travels fast in a hospital. Three nurses, an orderly, and the dietitian were convened in the hall outside the treatment room, and they pounced on me. "Chief, we heard Patrice Gentry is dead," the dietitian said. "Is that true?"

"I'm afraid so," I told him. "Dr. Gentry's taking it pretty hard. Y'all know him?"

They all nodded firmly, to let me know they were *close* to the good doctor. "Poor man," the dietitian said. "He worshiped that woman."

This seemed to agree with what the others knew of him, but it wasn't what I'd hoped to hear. "I don't believe I've ever seen a man so upset. Boy, I sure hope it's not one of those times when there's been a spat and they didn't have time to make up." That was meant to be an opening. You know: hint a little and see what pops out of tight mouths.

"I wouldn't think so," one of the nurses said, as if she wanted to set the record straight. "Patrice told me they never leave the room until they've settled an argument. Something they saw in an old movie once."

"You know he'd send her flowers sometimes, for no reason at all."

"Well, that's good to know. I guess he's just torn up 'cause he loved her, then. Not many husbands or wives either can say that after a few years of marriage." What, cynical? Me?

The dietitian, who seemed the oldest one there

and probably the longest married, chuckled. "Ain't that the truth? I never seen a couple like this one, though. That Patrice Gentry has been taking care of my grandma over at the nursing home. She's an angel, an absolute angel."

"They were a perfect match," the orderly said, and the others nodded agreement.

Well, how often does this happen? I wondered. Clearly I would need to dig deeper to get any dirt on the Gentrys, so I did what any sensible investigator would do under the circumstances.

"Reb, are you still wanderin' around?" That's the first thing Eloise said when I walked into the diner. She whipped out a mug and poured it full of coffee, plunked it down on the counter, and added, "Sit down and tell me about it. I've already heard it's Patrice Gentry, and her husband's taking it hard. Somebody shot her in her car? What is this, Miami? We're not safe on the streets?"

"Aha," I said. "She wasn't on the street, she was in a parking lot."

"Well, mercy. I feel better *now*." Eloise lit up one of those long brown cigarettes and pushed an ashtray over next to me for us to share. "What else have I missed?"

"Nothing, I hope. You know the Gentrys?"

"Of course. I usually see Patrice when I pop over of an evening to visit Miss Constance. Real pretty, without being overdone."

"I wouldn't know. Never saw her until this morning. She didn't look so good at that point."

Eloise shook her head. "What a shame. You'll see

pictures of her, I guess, before you're finished. Dark hair and eyes, a sweet face with dimples when she smiled. Everybody says she's an angel and Miss Constance thinks the world of her."

That's the kind of information that can clear up a case right quick. Miss Constance liked the victim. Let's see ... what might that tell us about Patrice Gentry? Miss Constance Winter had kept a whole room in her house crammed full of rocks. Miss Constance believes it is socially acceptable to run naked through the halls of the nursing home every time she gets a winning poker hand. Miss Constance, who has been locked up in the home for the aged for well onto three years now is fond of telling us about her recent vacations to Tahiti, Australia, or Beirut. Hmmmm.

"Eloise," I said to her, "I've heard tell of cities where murder victims are scum of the earth and where the killers are found standing over the bodies, gun in hand, shouting, 'I did it! I killed him!' Now, how come nothing like that ever happens here in Jesus Creek?"

She gave me that sideways, where's-your-head-boy look and said, "Hell, Reb. You're starting to talk like the Yankees that move in here, wanting to know why Jesus Creek can't be like wherever it is they come from. You don't want to be *ordinary*, do you?"

Sometimes, yeah. Didn't mention it to Eloise, though. Didn't seem safe.

"So Patrice Gentry was a fine lady. Anything else?" I finished my coffee, hoping Eloise would

take a hint and get to the point, if she had one,
about the Gentrys.

She refilled my cup. "Dr. Gentry is popular.
Haven't been to him myself, but Delia Cannon says
he was real gentle and friendly when he set her
broken ankle. Most of the mothers around town are
tickled to death with the way he handles their kids.
Anybody who can put up with colicky, measle-y,
ear-infected, screaming kids gets my vote. Speaking of votes, did you hear who's running for
mayor?"

Ever notice how the woman talks in twelve directions at once? "Patrick McCullough. Thanks for re-
minding me."

"Got a new candidate just this morning. Looks
like Patrick's gonna have a hard time this election."

Be still my heart! I had a sudden burst of opti-
mism, thinking we were going to get ourselves a
real mayor at last. "Who is it?" I foolishly asked.

"Henry Mooten." Mind you, she said this with a
straight face, as if Henry were a serious contender.
"He said he doesn't much care for politics and
hadn't had a thought of running for office until just
last week. Seems he spent a couple of months trying to get someone from the city council to listen to
him. They kept referring him to Patrick, who'd
send him to first one county office then another. So
Henry told me this morning he'd decided the only
way to get it built was to become mayor. He figures
Howard Baker and Al Gore sort of cleared the path
for Tennesseans in government."

"Get what built?" I asked, knowing in my heart
that all was lost.

"The landing pad," Eloise said, and blew a puff of smoke up toward the ceiling. "For the UFOs."

I stopped at the PD on my way home and left word for German to check on Steve Gentry, see if he was in any shape to talk. Should have had him question everybody again, I guess, but by that time my head was too fuzzy to think straight. I'd meant to get right to sleep, but I thought it might be a good idea to relax a little before I went off to bed, so I stripped down to my shorts and had a snack in front of the TV. Dozed off first thing, of course, and didn't wake up till nearly ten o'clock. This shift's killing me.

So after a shower and a big bowl of Frosted Flakes, I decided to go ahead and cruise town. Which took all of two minutes. Kay was pulling in to Eloise's when I drove past, so I circled around and joined her, thinking I'd catch up on what had been happening during the day, maybe fill her in on what I wanted to get done as soon as possible in the Gentry case. She'd seen me coming and had a cup of coffee waiting for me.

It still makes me do a double take when I see her in uniform. How on earth do you suppose a little bitty girl like her made it through the academy? She's real proud of it, of course. Unlike some of the rest of us, Kay always has creases in her pants and a spit shine on her badge.

"I feel like I'm living with my parents," she said as soon as I came in.

"Why's that?"

"You're checking up on me again."

Absolutely not true. Yeah, I worry about having a woman working nights alone, but damned if I'm gonna baby-sit her. And I've told her that a few dozen times already. In her own special way, Kay's just as aggravating as German.

"You know all about Patrice Gentry?" I said, ignoring her accusation.

Kay nodded and pulled out her notebook. "German looked around at the scene and didn't find anything unusual. Windshield glass, a smashed ballpoint pen with red ink, an empty food wrapper. Dr. Gentry had been sedated by the time German got to him, so he was calm. Here." She handed me a stack of typed pages—the statement that German had taken from Dr. Gentry.

"I'll go over it later," I said, rolling the papers into a cylinder and sticking them in my back pocket. "Unless there's something I need to know right away." I felt sure Kay would have memorized the statement before she handed it over to me.

"No, not a thing. So far," she added ominously. "Hubby had a fainting spell before *I* got much talking done. I'll get back to him first thing in the morning if there's any question about his statement."

"Maybe you should have caught him when he came to. He might have been more vulnerable to questioning then. *If* he really fainted."

"Shoot, Kay. If you'd told me he was the guilty party, I'd have just arrested him on the spot. Silly me. I was giving the guy a chance to get over the shock of his wife's death." I slapped my forehead and groaned. "If only I'd been fresh out of the academy instead of a veteran officer of umpteen years."

"Did I say he did it? I only meant to suggest that everyone is a suspect at this point." Kay spews out this kind of Joe Friday philosophy all the time. I remember when German used to do that. At the time I wanted to cram a sock in his mouth, but now that he's talking about heart-shaped candelabra and cummerbunds, I almost miss the tough-cop lingo.

"Don't be sarcastic, Reb," Kay said. "I've been making a pass by the Gentrys' house every hour or so. Those people must have known everybody in town and then some. Cars parked all up and down the street, and in the yard. Whatever shape Gentry's in, he's got plenty of people to support him."

"That's good. A man needs his friends at a time like this. I'll hang around a couple of hours in the morning, try to catch him at home at a decent hour. Don't expect he'll be going to work for a while yet. At least not until after her funeral." The cereal was starting to wear off, so I motioned for the waitress to come on over. "I expect I'll have to talk to everybody who worked with Patrice, plus the neighbors. You'd think, wouldn't you, that somebody would have had a grudge against her."

"Well, I never met her," Kay said, "but everyone says she was an angel."

"Hell, yes. *Every*one says that very thing. But I can't believe she's gone through life without ticking off at least one person somewhere."

"People can be wonderful, Reb. Look at Wayne."

Ah, the tunnel vision of young lovers. In addition to German's wedding plans, I've been hearing lots more than I want to know about Wayne Holland. To hear Kay tell it, he's a saint. The ideal man. Compared to the ones she's gotten tangled up with before, I imagine he's a big step up, but wouldn't you think her own history would scare the daylights out of her?

"If you want to be useful, why don't you run by the nursing home tomorrow afternoon and talk to the evening-shift nurses? Find out everything they know about Patrice Gentry. In particular, find out if any of them hated her and planned a little surprise in a dark parking lot last night."

Kay perked right up, thrilled to have an honest-to-gosh police assignment. "I could go over there now and catch them as they're leaving work."

"For God's sake, no," I said. "Then you'd want to stay up all night discussing it with me, and I plan to pull the car up under a tree somewhere and get some sleep tonight."

"You sleep on duty?" She was honestly surprised.

Fortunately Roger and Delia decided to join us for a minute on their way out and saved me from having to lie in order to set a good example for my officer.

"Reb, I've heard about Patrice Gentry," Delia said, without even a friendly greeting first. "Do you have any idea who's responsible?"

"The investigation is proceeding steadily," I told her.

"I certainly hope it is. Patrice was a lovely lady. What a tragedy."

"Delia formed an instant bond with Patrice,"

Roger explained, "when she learned that Patrice was the other vegetarian in Jesus Creek."

"Is that right?" Kay said, jotting that information down in her notebook.

"Vegan," Delia added.

"Isn't that where Henry Mooten's aliens come from? Vega?"

"Vegan means Patrice didn't eat meat *or* dairy products *or* eggs," Delia said.

"Vegetarianism is dangerous, don't ya know? Didn't you hear about that woman up in Montana? Married a real he-man type, reformed him, turned him into a vegetarian, too. Guy used to be big into hunting, but he sold all his guns for her. So one day she takes him out on a camping trip. Buys a fortune's worth of cameras and equipment and says that's how they shoot animals from now on. Third day of the trip, husband drives into the nearest town, screaming about how a bunch of hunters shot his wife by accident. Sure enough, her body's back at the campsite, dead as can be."

"Hunting accidents happen to meat eaters, too, Reb," Delia pointed out.

"There's more. The police found her journal, in which she'd mentioned how nice it was to be enjoying the peacefulness of a protected wilderness *where hunters weren't allowed to roam.* Shortly after that, they found the gun—the one hubby didn't sell—hidden in a crevice not far from the campsite. Found traces of gunpowder on the husband's hands and nailed him."

"I always suspected cholesterol deprivation would have that effect on a man," Roger put in.

I made a mental note to check the contents of the Gentrys' refrigerator, see if the good doctor had purchased a large amount of red meat since his wife's death.

I looked over Gentry's statement while eating a piece of the best chocolate pie Eloise has turned out so far. Beats me why she can't hold on to a husband. You'd think a man would put up with a lot to get food like that every day.

The sedative Gentry had been given might have calmed him down, but not by much. Even reading a transcript of the conversation, I could tell he was fairly well devastated by his wife's death. Or wanted us to believe he was. You never know.

Gentry had said he'd last seen his wife at noon, when she'd come by his office with sandwiches for lunch. They'd talked about ordinary married-type matters, then she'd gone home to change for work.

He also said that while he'd expected her home a little after eleven P.M., he'd gone on to bed early that night. The next thing he knew, it was morning and he was hurrying to the emergency room, in response to a call from one of his pregnant patients.

Dull, if you ask me. If he needed an alibi, that wasn't much of one.

By midnight, I'd pulled up behind the library and was just dozing off when the radio squawked. Al was about as excited as he's ever been, and he'd already hollered for me three times before I could grab the mike and answer.

"Chief!" he said, loud enough to wake the dead.

I turned down the volume and assured him that I was listening.

"There's been a robbery over on Morning Glory. At the Veatch place. They've just come home and they saw the guy running away!"

Wouldn't you know it? Not more than once a month do I ever get a call on midnight shift, and this one has to be the night I, number one, need sleep and, number two, am napping less than fifty yards from the crime scene.

The Veatches were waiting for me on the front porch. He was already making out a list of missing items, and she was practically jumping up and down. I don't think I've seen her that excited since the time the squirrel got loose in their house.

"Everybody's okay, I guess," I said to them.

"We're fine!" she told me. "But we saw him! We saw him!"

Mr. Veatch nodded, and it did my heart a world of good. I mean, can you think of anybody in this world more likely to give you a detailed, accurate, and complete description of the suspect than Eagle-Eye Veatch?

"The French doors in back have been smashed," Mrs. Veatch said. "With this crowbar. It's not ours." She held out the bar, which she'd carefully lifted with one finger wrapped in a dishtowel. "Do you think there might be prints?"

"Could be," I said, thinking, Not a chance. I took the bar and the towel and placed both on the passenger seat in my car, then rejoined the Veatches on the porch to get the rest of the story.

"Now," I said, and whipped out my notebook, "what'd he look like?"

"Young," Veatch said. "Probably a teenager. About five feet six inches tall, not more than one hundred twenty pounds, I'd say. Wearing jeans and a denim jacket. He had a backpack. Can't be sure about hair color. Dark blond or light brown."

"Don't suppose it was anybody you recognized?"

Veatch shook his head. "I don't know young people."

"I know scads of them," Mrs. Veatch offered, "but not this one. I don't think."

"Was he on foot or driving a car?"

Mr. Veatch pointed back behind the house, toward Primrose Lane. "He ran on foot in that direction. Could have had a car parked over there. I haven't heard any engines except yours, though."

I jotted all that down, thinking that it probably wouldn't be as useful as I'd first hoped. We've got a lot of teenagers in this town, after all. "What all did he take?"

"Oh, nothing important," Mrs. Veatch said. She didn't seem concerned about the loss of property, just hyped about having walked in on a crime-in-progress.

Looking at his list, Mr. Veatch said, "The VCR, a portable tape player, some cash that was left out on the dresser"—he gave his wife a meaningful look—"and three Alabama tapes."

"And he had all this in his hands when he took off?" I asked.

"More likely in the backpack. Of course, there

may be other items missing. I haven't had time to look closely."

"Tell you the truth, Mr. Veatch," I said, "we probably won't be able to get any of this back for you. You be sure to call your insurance company right away and report this."

He handed me a sheet of paper. "Serial number for the tape player and VCR," he said. "I'll check the house again, and if I find anything else missing, I'll get back to you." Turning to his wife, he asked her, "Can you talk to the insurance agent tomorrow?"

"Oh, sure," she said. "I have to get my roots done at ten, and then I'll take care of it."

Veatch gave me a tight little smile and wished me a quieter night.

By the time I got back to the car, I wasn't sleepy anymore. The robbery bugged me. The Veatches were the third family in three months to get hit, and while that doesn't exactly constitute a crime wave, it sure seemed like more than enough. The other two houses were empty, both had had windows or doors smashed, but the tool used to break the glass had never been left behind before. I figured the kid must have forgotten to retrieve it in his hurry to get away when the Veatches surprised him. Fingerprints sure would be useful, but I've learned it's never a good idea to count on a criminal's stupidity. Oh, sure. They pull some pretty dumb stunts, but never *that* dumb.

All the same, I took the crowbar into PD and tagged it. I let Al check it for prints, because he doesn't have much in his life, and I filled out half a dozen forms.

After that, I pulled up the files on those other two robberies. Strangest damned list. So far, among the missing, we could count a folding camp stool, a computer, a portable phone, a beat-up old coffeepot (the kind you put on top of the stove), jewelry, money, some fishing gear, and—from the Tuesday-night robbery at the Sikeses' house—a Colt 2000, with fitted case. The gun was loaded when it was stolen and the thief had not taken the extra magazine, even though Sikes kept *that* right with the gun.

Well, it's sure the most peculiar series of thefts I've ever seen. Almost like somebody's stealing for fun and not for gain. All the burglaries were committed while the homeowners were out of town, not just out of the house. In each case, entry had been through the back door, and the thief had pried open both storm and interior doors of the sort that just have a little push-button lock.

Enough similarities that it could well have been the same person, but with only three break-ins and one description of the suspect, I didn't want to jump to conclusions. I figured Kay could do that.

CHAPTER
3

In the time of man's innocence

SO MUCH FOR CATCHING UP ON MY SLEEP.

I drove past Gentry's house a couple of times, way on up in the wee hours, and both times there was a little red Honda sitting in the driveway. It seemed to me like Gentry had had enough time to pull himself together, so I decided I'd get over there and question him before I went home.

I stoked up on coffee at the PD for the last hour of my shift. Then German came in and started yapping about music for the wedding reception. You know, the one time I got married, we just went to the courthouse with a couple of friends along to witness the mistake, we said a few words, and that was it. No fuss. Shoot, German's wedding won't be paid for until after the divorce!

I listened to as much of him as I could stand, then excused myself to get out to the Gentrys' neighborhood. Figured if I got there early enough, I might catch Dr. Gentry's neighbors before they left for work, or wherever they spent their days.

You've seen the Gentry house, I guess. It's that big brick place that sits back off the road, right next to where Oliver Host's house used to be. Fairly

secluded now that the Host house has burned, with
just the one set of neighbors. Big lawn, but way too
many flowers. Lot of trouble to mow around, but I
guess the Gentrys expect to hire somebody to do
that for them. They haven't spent a summer in Jesus Creek yet. Wait till they find out that nobody's
available to do the work for them, because we're all
so busy trying to keep our own grass cut.

Compared to the Gentrys' place, the Barrows' little square brick looked puny. Probably just as much
floor space, but built to look as much like a box as
possible. Brown trim, a couple of evergreen shrubs
on either side of the front door. The only decoration
I could find was a Christmas wreath still hanging
on the front door.

I pushed the doorbell button, but since I've never
yet encountered a doorbell that works, I went
ahead and knocked. One or the other got attention,
'cause in just a minute the door opened and there
stood Anne Barrow, all decked out in a power suit.
Women look scary in those getups, and it's not because I'm nervous about women taking control, either. I think it's because those stiff-shouldered
suits and high-heeled shoes always seem to be part
of a set that includes a whip.

"Chief Gassler," she said, and stepped back to let
me in. "I expected you to drop by. Come on in.
Would you like coffee?"

I told her truthfully that coffee just might save
my life, so she led me back to the kitchen and
poured us out a cup each, before offering me a seat
at the breakfast table. First time in my life I've
ever been uncomfortable in a kitchen. This one was

beyond spartan. White walls, white cabinets and appliances, not a crayon portrait or grocery list in sight. The whole place looked like an institution, designed for easy cleanup. I guess that's how a mind like Anne Barrow's works, though—straight and sterile and logical. How else could she make a living writing computer programs?

"James left early this morning," she said, "but if you need to talk to him, you can drop by his office."

"I'll try not to bother him at work if I can help it," I said. "Any chance he'll be around this afternoon?"

She nodded. "He'll be late—he can never seem to get his work finished on time—but I expect him before eight o'clock, or so. In the meantime I can tell you that I haven't noticed anything unusual at the Gentrys'. Patrice and I spoke briefly last weekend and she seemed fine to me."

"Any reason she shouldn't have been fine?"

Anne shook her head. "I only meant that she didn't seem worried or upset, as she might have if she'd had trouble with someone. Trouble enough to cause her death, that is."

"Were you and Mrs. Gentry good friends?"

"Yes, I'd say we were. Not terribly close, as in lunching or shopping together. But I was quite fond of her. She's helped me through some difficult times in my life. And I believe she was fond of me."

"Seems everybody liked Mrs. Gentry," I said. "So far, I haven't heard a word against her."

"Patrice was very kind. I don't know if they'd wanted children and hadn't been able to have any, or if childlessness was a conscious choice for some reason, but Patrice adored little ones. She's like a second mother to my two, and probably to others. You know she works with Special Olympics?"

I hadn't known that, but it didn't surprise me. "Did a lot of volunteer work, did she?" I jotted down a reminder to talk to the folks who handle Special Olympics in Angela County.

"A lot for someone with a full-time job. Once a week she delivered for Meals on Wheels. Steve can tell you everything, I'm sure."

"Dr. Gentry kept close tabs on his wife?"

"He didn't keep tabs on her, Chief. He was an important part of her life, so naturally he knew what her interests were. If you think Steve had anything to do with his wife's death, you're absolutely wrong. He was totally devoted to her."

"So I hear. Must have been hard on him, though, what with his long hours keeping him away from home, and her evening shift tying up her nights."

"I'm sure they made time to be together, Chief. Sometimes Steve would meet her after she got off work and they'd drive down to the river for a picnic by moonlight. When Patrice told me about that, I thought it was wonderfully romantic. In fact, that's what I thought they were doing the night she was killed."

"Why did you think that?" I asked.

"Well, I heard Steve's car pull in around midnight. I assumed Patrice was right behind him, so it occurred to me they might have been picnicking. Just a thought that passed through my head at the time."

I finished off my coffee and stood to leave. "I ap-

preciate your help, Mrs. Barrow," I said. "Don't let
me make you late for work. Tell your husband I'll
get back to him."

She walked me to the door, gave me a cordial
farewell, and closed the door the minute I was off
the front step. Nothing wrong there, except that
Anne Barrow always gives me the willies. Is it natural for a woman to be so cool? I don't believe I've
ever seen a trace of emotion out of her.

The house, the yard—all of it was just as barren.
A stranger could drive by that house and assume it
had been empty for years. Next door, the Gentrys'
yard was landscaped and greening from the spring
sun, with promises of flowers to come. And a little
farther down the road was the Weldons' place—
leaning toward shabby, but full of kids' toys and
scattered flowers and bushes.

The Barrows could have been some alien family
that had moved to Earth but hadn't quite gotten
the hang of living human yet. I'd have to mention
that to Henry.

A glance at Steve Gentry's driveway told me the
red Honda's owner hadn't left yet. I kind of liked
that. Call me curious, but I looked forward to finding out who'd spent the night in Gentry's house.
And then you could have knocked me over with a
feather when she came walking out the front door
just as I was about to knock.

"What are you doing here?" she asked, startled
half out of her skin when she saw me.

"You're Gentry's nurse. I came in the other morning—"

"I remember," she said. "But you can't bother

him. Dr. Gentry is still terribly upset about his wife's death."

"Is he, now?" I asked, wondering how upset he'd been all through the night. "I sure hate to bother him, but if we're ever gonna catch the killer, we need his help. Now, if you'll excuse me, I'll just go on in."

She looked like she was about to bar the door, but I pushed past her. Still, she didn't give up easily. She trotted on ahead of me, calling out, "Dr. Gentry? There's someone here to see you."

She was headed for the back of the house, so I followed her, thinking she'd surely know where the man was. It could have been awkward, I suppose, but I didn't mind putting a little pressure on the doctor. I was disappointed to find him sitting at his kitchen table, fully dressed, and drinking coffee.

"Sorry to bother you, sir," I said to Gentry. "I wish this could wait, but I've put it off as long as I can. I'll need some help from you—"

"Of course," Gentry said. "Anything you need. I want you to find the person who hurt Patrice."

Get that? The person who hurt Patrice?

He looked up at the nurse and gave her a big smile. "Go ahead, Amanda. I'll call later if I need anything. And thanks so much for everything you did last night."

Amanda threw me one last warning look and left. I was preoccupied, wondering exactly what she'd done for him last night, but Gentry's mind was amazingly clear for a man who should have still been feeling the effects of that nerve pill he'd been given.

"I'm just double-checking, sir," I told him. "Maybe you've remembered something since my deputy took your statement. Now that you've had time to calm down."

"I want you to understand," he said, "that Patrice was a wonderful woman. Everyone adored her. Whatever happened, it wasn't intended for her."

"You mean you don't think she was a target in particular?"

"Absolutely not," Gentry insisted. "Perhaps in the course of a random robbery, or even a random shooting, she happened to be in the wrong place. I realize this makes it more difficult to catch the guilty party, but I hope you will make every effort, Chief."

"Oh, you can count on that, Dr. Gentry," I said sincerely. "I fully intend to find out who killed your wife." I took my time about getting the notebook from my pocket and opening it to a clean page. "Now, sir," I went on, "when your wife didn't come home on time Wednesday night, did you call the nursing home to check on her?"

"Oh, no." Gentry shook his head, as if I'd misunderstood something he'd said. "Patrice often worked an extra shift, so I naturally assumed that's what she was doing that night. With my hours, I'm often asleep before then anyway, so she wouldn't have called."

"I see," I said, real casual. "And were you asleep Wednesday night?"

Gentry thought about it for a minute, then said, "Why, yes. I suppose I would have been asleep by the end of her shift. I'd had a tough day and I remember I just crashed as soon as I got home. Slept right through until the alarm went off the next morning. I had to be at the Med Center early, because I was pulling emergency that day and we delivered a baby about seven-thirty that morning. Then, of course, you arrived. . . ." His voice trailed off and his eyes started to fill up with tears.

Not that it mattered. Gentry didn't have to tell me anything else. If he claimed he'd been home in bed when his wife was killed, and the neighbor claimed she'd heard his car pull into the driveway around midnight, somebody was lying.

It was only a little after eight, but diligent Amanda's car was parked in the staff-only parking lot. I never understood why old Doc Porter had his office between the grocery store and the Wash-O-Rama, and I surely don't know why Gentry took the place over, instead of getting one of those nice, quiet buildings over on Morning Glory, but there you are. Try to figure out doctors or lawyers and it'll drive you nuts.

The sign on the front door said CLOSED UNTIL FURTHER NOTICE, and it was topped off by a fancy wreathful of flowers I couldn't identify and probably couldn't pay for with a month's salary. I pounded on the door hard enough to wake the dead, just in case Amanda was in the back or something. In a little bit she peeked out at me through the glass pane and mouthed, "We're closed." I shook my head to let her know I wasn't going anywhere and I do believe she mouthed something else before unlocking the door to let me in.

"Dr. Gentry won't be in today," she said, and started to close the door.

"I've finished with him for the day," I told her. "Right now I'd like a word with you. If you don't mind."

I could tell she didn't like it, but she opened the door enough for me to squeeze through. I was surprised to see the molded plastic chairs Gentry put in the waiting room. This was the first time I'd been in the office since Gentry took over, and it sure didn't look the same as when Doc Porter was around. Remember that black-and-white tile floor that was harder than concrete? Now that's been covered up with a pink carpet (probably called mauve) and the pad underneath must be six inches thick. Felt like walking on a ship in stormy seas. There's a bunch of ferns hanging down from the ceiling, and pretty little pictures on the walls, and even new magazines on the glass tables. I looked around for one of Doc Porter's ashtrays, but I guess that's just not done anymore.

"Chief, I have to apologize for my manner this morning," she said, coming to a halt in front of me so fast I almost knocked her down. "It hasn't been easy for any of us here, and Dr. Gentry is beside himself. I didn't mean to be short with you. I simply wanted to save him as much trouble as possible."

"I understand that," I told her. "And I don't want to cause problems, but I've got to have answers if I'm going to solve Patrice Gentry's murder."

"Yes, of course. Why don't you come on back here? I can give you a few minutes, but not much

longer. We're catching up on our backlog while the
office is closed. Genny," she said to the receptionist,
"the Chief and I are going to talk in Dr. Gentry's office."

The biggest examining room has been turned
into the doctor's office. It's paneled in oak, and a
great big window takes up most of one wall. Gentry's desk is made of some sort of wood that's probably grown in a rain forest, and the chair behind it
looked to be genuine leather. I couldn't believe Delia Cannon, defender of the earth and its children,
approved of the guy.

"The doctor is terribly upset. Losing Mrs. Gentry
has been devastating. I've taken the liberty of can-
celing appointments for the next week, and I may
have to cancel even more. There's just no way of
telling if he'll be able to resume his practice before
he leaves for Somalia." Poor Amanda plucked a
pink tissue from the box on the table and sniffed
into it. Then she made herself comfy in the doctor's
chair.

"Somalia?" I asked. This was a new one.

"Oh, yes. Dr. and Mrs. Gentry were finalizing
plans for a mercy mission. It's their way of showing
gratitude for the many bounties in their lives.
They've done this often, in different countries
where the need for medical personnel is overwhelming."

"I don't understand why Dr. Gentry didn't have
his wife working for him here at the clinic," I said.
"I'm sure you're a fine nurse, but—"

"No, I understand why you'd ask," Amanda assured me. "They considered that, in fact. But Dr.

Gentry told me when he hired me that his wife was especially interested in geriatric medicine. Often, when they were in underdeveloped countries, she'd felt at a loss when dealing with the older residents of a village. She had specialized in pediatrics, you see."

I didn't think she'd have found all that many old people in those countries. Who lives to be an adult in Somalia? "I guess Dr. Finster will have a heavy load until you get a replacement for Gentry," I said.

"Yes, and I've asked for the loan of two interns from Nashville to handle emergency cases in the meantime. Dr. Gentry does a great deal more than most people realize."

"Working all day, and running to the hospital during the night. It's a wonder he's not exhausted," I sympathized.

"The only thing that keeps him going is his devotion to healing," Amanda said with a straight face. "He and Mrs. Gentry had that in common."

"Did you know Mrs. Gentry real well? Or just in passing?"

"Oh, I knew her fairly well. She was in and out of the office, and of course I spoke to her on the phone often when she'd call. An outstanding nurse, from all I've heard. I know Dr. Gentry was very proud of her."

"I hear she'd worked for some charities. Do you know if Dr. Gentry did anything like that?"

"Not officially," she said, as if confiding state secrets, "but several times he's asked us to give a discounted rate to patients who aren't able to pay the full price. Without mentioning it to them, of course, because Dr. Gentry wouldn't want to hurt their feelings or make them feel like charity cases."

"Thoughtful man. Next you'll be telling me he still makes house calls."

"Once in a while, when it isn't convenient for the patient to come in," she admitted. "I've tried to discourage him from doing that, but Dr. Gentry believes in giving personal care to his patients. For him, that includes knowing the names of all their children, and listening to all their tales of woe. It's a compassionate form of healing, but it does drain a lot of his energy."

"He was actually out on some kind of call the night his wife was killed, wasn't he?" I asked her.

"He may have been," Amanda said grudgingly.

"Do you remember which patient he was with that night?"

Amanda turned a sharp-eyed look on me. "If you're suggesting that Dr. Gentry needs an alibi for that night, you're way out of line. And if you want to check up on him, you'll have to do it somewhere else. I won't be a party to this."

"I'm asking questions in a calm and pleasant manner. There's no need for you to get your tail feathers in a knot. Now, can you just look in the records and tell me who Dr. Gentry saw that night?" I wondered if she'd lie to protect Gentry. I'd even given her a story, and for a minute it looked as if she'd go for it, but then . . .

Amanda leaned forward with her hands on the desk like she was about to propel herself over it and straight at me. "All right, Chief Gassler," she said. "If you must know, I was with Dr. Gentry on Wednesday night. Does that satisfy you?"

"I see," I said. "Well, I don't suppose that surprises me. Still, I'm just going to ask you—are you absolutely certain it was Wednesday night?"

"Yes." She nodded firmly. "He was with me all night. Now, if you don't mind, I have a lot of work to do." She stood up and stalked back out to the front desk, leaving me to find my own way out. She didn't wave goodbye, either.

I'd kind of suspected something was going on between Amanda and the doctor, especially since she'd obviously and without shame spent the night with him. What I couldn't figure out was, if they were that indiscreet, how come nobody else had mentioned it? The whole town must have been in on the secret.

I pondered that on my way out to the car. I also thought some about Gentry's financial situation. A doctor who gives discount rates out of the goodness of his heart didn't sound quite right to me, but maybe he was independently wealthy. Or maybe he was counting on a hefty life-insurance policy to make up the difference.

I made a quick stop at the PD and put in a call to Sheriff Barlow, asking for some help with the investigation of Patrice Gentry's murder.

"Sure thing," he said. "We got nothing better to do."

I knew, of course, that this was sarcasm. Barlow's four-man force is more overworked than mine,

and their cars are always losing bits and pieces out
on those bumpy county roads.

"Here's where we are," I told him. "Medical examiner's got the body, but he's backlogged, so it'll
be a while before we get the complete report. The
TBI's mobile van won't be operational for a couple
more weeks, so we won't get more than sporadic
help from them. And the district attorney said he'd
just as soon we not find the killer, since he's up to
his eyeballs in work already."

"In other words," Barlow drawled, "you want me
to take a wild guess, arrest somebody, do the
paperwork, prosecute him, then hang him from a
tree. Glad to help. I'd hate to put the rest of you to
any trouble."

"Well, what else you got to do besides sit on your
hairy butt and get older?" I asked. "So I'll drop off
the information we've got later today. Let me know
if you have any bright ideas. We'd all like to see
what happens when you finally put your brain in
gear."

Barlow's a good man. I knew he'd do all he could
to help, but he had his own job to take care of, too.
I expect he's like me—pushing a big old boulder up
the side of a hill, with a team of goats trying to
push it back down on him.

I left German a list of things to do, including getting hold of those financial records for the Gentrys
and passing those, as well as everything else, along
to Barlow. And then, just because I'm trying to del-
egate more, I left a message for Kay to go by the
Barrows around eight P.M. and question James. After that, having no one I wanted to visit with (when

are you coming home?), I decided to do brunch at
Eloise's.

A sad sight met me at the front door. Henry
Mooten and his little friends were coloring up
poster board with Magic Markers, trying to turn
them into campaign signs. Hell, those VOTE FOR
CLINTON AND GORE signs haven't come down yet. I
saw one the other day, stapled to a light pole out on
Dead Branch Road. Now we're gonna have Henry's
artwork tackying up the landscape.

But just in case he wins, I figured I'd better keep
on his good side, so I joined Henry and Frank and
the gang at their table. "Morning, boys," I said.
"Hear you threw your hat in the ring, Henry."

Henry nodded without looking up from the poster
he was working on. "Somebody's got to."

I thought it best not to come right out and say
one way or the other, but I sure agree that McCullough's got to be kicked out of office soon. Truth be
told, I'm not sure Henry wouldn't be better. He may
not have good sense, but at least he's earnest.
McCullough's so shallow, if he was a creek you were
crossing, you wouldn't even get the top of your foot
wet.

"We're starting the Common Sense party," Frank
Pate said, and the other men nodded agreement.
"Low-cost campaign, based on honesty, integrity,
and genuine concern for the community."

I wasn't sure how UFO landing pads fit the com-
monsense part, but of course I agreed with the rest.

"Got this pretty well mapped out, have you?"

"Get out. Talk to people. Find out what they really want, instead of telling 'em what they *ought* to

want. Henry's already laid out plans for the landing pad. And we were just thinking about something more social. Say, an official sister city for Jesus Creek. Any ideas?"

"Mirabeau, Texas," Eloise said, setting the cup down in front of me.

"Where's that?" Henry asked, looking up from his poster.

"Well, I'm not exactly sure, but my second cousin's been there a few years now, and she just loves that little town."

Henry nodded and Frank wrote the name of the town on his list. "How about you, Reb? You see more of this town than the rest of us put together. What do you want changed?"

"Bigger budget for the police department wouldn't hurt. As it stands, there's five of us working ourselves half to death. Now, that wasn't so bad a few years ago. When I first joined the force here, crime was when somebody's dog got shot by a careless deer hunter. Times have changed." I realized *I* sounded like a politician, trying to persuade these fellows over to my way of thinking. "The world caught up with us here in Jesus Creek."

"Damned shame about that," Frank said, but nobody disagreed with me. "Maybe that's something to discuss with folks, Henry. See how they feel about getting back to the old days. Use that family-values issue."

Henry looked up toward the ceiling, maybe checking with his celestial advisory board. "Yep. I reckon everybody'll go for that. Trouble's gettin' 'em to agree on what *family values* means."

Frank thought about it for a second and suggested, "Respect for others. The Golden Rule. That's what we oughta stress. What we need is a political platform that's based on the Golden Rule."

I wouldn't mind finding a political philosophy based on *The Beverly Hillbillies*, myself. Oh, sure. Laugh. You're like all these folks who think that show was a comedy about some barefoot hillbillies who made fools of themselves in the big city. Look again, I say. Who was the biggest fool on that program? How about Banker Drysdale, always grubbing for money and selling his mother or his soul for a sweet deal? Compare him to that feisty young Jethro, who dreamed dreams and went after them, pure of heart. Ellie May should be the feminist poster child. She loved animals more than men, which seems reasonable to me, and never backed down from nobody when she knew she was right. Poor old Granny struggled just to survive, and never turned bitter or resentful. And when you needed her medicine, she was there to help, no matter who you might be.

When it comes to great philosophers, nobody can touch Jed Clampett. Sit down in front of your set someday, watch three or four episodes of that show, and listen to what Uncle Jed's saying. If you live by his advice, you're guaranteed some happiness on earth and a pair of wings later on.

"You fellas ever been to Dr. Gentry?" I asked, while considering what I'd have from the menu.

"Once," Frank said. "Nice man. Real good doctor, too. Everybody says. That pretty little wife of his does a fine job of taking care of the old folks out at the nursing home, too. From what I hear, the Gentrys are a mighty fine pair. Awful sad about what happened, idn' it?"

"Gentry ever make a house call for you?" I asked, still skeptical about that claim.

"Nope," Frank said, "but he come out to Benny and Chester once, when they both got down with the flu. Brought his wife with him, and she made sure Benny and Chester got a good, hot meal, and then she straightened up around the house for 'em."

Listening to Frank, I thought maybe I'd missed something important about the Gentrys. It sounded as if Jed Clampett and clan had reincarnated, not in TV syndication land, but right here in Jesus Creek.

CHAPTER

4

Honorable among all men

ELOISE CALLED MY NAME AND HELD THE
phone receiver out to me.

"Can't a man find peace anywhere?" I grumbled,
but went on around behind the cash register to
take the call.

"Chief, I need you back at the PD," German said.

"I just left there. And my message was perfectly
clear. All you have to do is check bank records for
the Gentrys—"

"That's not it, Chief. You'd better come see for
yourself."

Eloise just smiled and shook her head, and sent
my sausage gravy back to the kitchen. "Don't lose
it," I told her on my way out the door. "I'll be back."

By the time I got to the office, German was
backed up against the wall by a tiny little woman
with great big hair. She was giving him what-for,
and he was taking it. Probably good training for
marriage.

"Look, miss," he said, trying to regain his compo-
sure, "this here's the man you need to talk to.
Chief, this woman's a little upset—"

"I'm not upset, you twit! I'm damned furious!

What's the matter with you people?" She spun
around and poked a finger at my chest, which I did
not care for.

Pushing her hand away, I tried staring her down.
It should have been easy, since she was more than
a foot shorter than me and about a third my
weight, but she didn't budge. "Okay, ma'am," I said.
"Let's just back up here and find out what the problem is. Now, first of all, what's your name?"

She kind of shook herself back into place and
gave me one more killer look. "I'm Teresa Simmons," she said. "And I want to know why you're
accusing Steve Gentry of killing his wife."

"Dr. Gentry hasn't been accused of anything," I
pointed out.

"Practically. You've been going all over town, asking questions about where he was that night and
whether he and Patrice were having problems. Everybody knows what you're thinking."

"I'm thinking that an investigation involves
questioning people. Would you like to tell me why
you, in particular, are so fired up that you've come
in here and terrorized my officer?" I glanced over at
German, who seemed appropriately embarrassed
by that comment. Serves him right. He should have
had the situation under control.

"If you want answers, you can start with me. I
know for a fact that Steve Gentry had nothing to do
with his wife's murder. He was with me that
night."

German and Bill both gawked, and truth be told,
my mouth might have dropped open a few inches.

"You're having an affair with Dr. Gentry?" I asked her.

"That's right," she said defiantly. "And he was with me the night his wife died. Okay?"

"Would you like to sit down here and give us a full statement?" I asked her. It didn't occur to me that she'd just complicated my investigation. I was only thinking of how much fun German and Bill were going to have listening to the conversation.

"Look," she said, somewhat calmer, "my husband has a temper. A vicious one. If he ever found out I'd been with Steve, he'd kill me. He'd probably kill Steve, too."

I didn't tell her we'd already had one woman claiming to have spent the night with Gentry, and considering how she'd put the fear of God into German, I didn't want to think what she'd do to poor little Amanda.

"So naturally I'd prefer to keep this quiet." She turned halfway around and gave German a meaningful glare. "But I'm telling you because I want you to leave Steve alone. I'm his alibi. That's all you need to know. But you've got to swear to keep this quiet."

I swore the tale would never leave that room. Foolish of her to believe that, since the walls have ears and German was bound to tell Pam, who surely would tell someone else, and so on. Gossip about this pair of lovebirds would be all over town before I could turn around twice.

I suggested to Mrs. Simmons that she tell her husband before somebody else enlightened him. I further suggested she make herself familiar with the domestic violence center, in case her husband really did try to kill her.

Furthermore I told her to seriously consider the penalty for lying to police in the course of a murder investigation, but that didn't faze her. She was probably more concerned about her husband—and rightly so.

You see what I was dealing with here? A married woman having an affair with a married man who may or may not have been sleeping with his nurse at the same time this other woman claims he was sleeping with her. And remember—I'd been up all night. Confused doesn't begin to describe how I felt.

"Now, if Gentry had been killed, I'd have a whole mess of suspects," I said to German. "His wife, these women he's been sleeping with. Some husband, maybe, or a boyfriend."

"Well, you could knock me over with a feather," Eloise said. "That nice man, running around on his wife. I never would have thought something like that." She set a fresh plate in front of me while shamelessly eavesdropping on what had now become my lunch conversation.

"I knew something had to be wrong with the man," I went on, speaking to German but making sure that Eloise could hear clearly. "Nobody's as perfect as he sounds. Hand me that saltshaker please." The warmed over sausage-gravy and biscuits would have suited me fine, but Eloise had insisted on fixing up a fresh plate, so I added a couple of fried eggs to the order. Lack of sleep was beginning to take its toll, though, and the food didn't taste nearly as good as it would have earlier.

"Well, which one do you think's telling the truth?" German asked, salting his own food before sharing the shaker. "Reckon the Simmons woman is just making it up? Looking for publicity?"

"Possible, but I'm more likely to believe Gentry's the liar. Incidentally, let this be a lesson. If you're gonna marry Pam, don't even think about cheating. She'd kill you in a heartbeat, and she's smart enough to get away with it." It was the only piece of marital advice I'd ever given to anyone, but I figured I couldn't go wrong by urging caution.

"Chief," German said, and blushed.

"I've left a message for Dr. Gentry, telling him I'll be at his house first thing in the morning. I want to hear how he explains coming in at midnight, and spending the night with a woman."

German grinned like I'd told a joke. "I can talk to him, Chief. If you want me to." He seemed to be hoping I would want that very thing.

Not likely, since I didn't trust German in his love-and-marriage daze to do much of anything. "I want you to concentrate on these break-ins. Check the pawnshops in the nearest counties. And why don't you pull the files on all the break-ins for the last six months or so?"

"No prob," German said, around a mouthful of fried potatoes.

"And don't forget to check the bank records for Gentry. And find out if Mrs. Gentry had a will, a life-insurance policy, whatever."

While I finished my food I mulled over the stories

I'd collected so far. Anne Barrow had said that Gentry got home around midnight the night his wife was murdered. That didn't fit with his story about staying home all night, *or* with either Teresa Simmons's or Amanda Brewer's claims that he'd been with them all night. At that point I wasn't even sure I could trust the victim to be dead.

I found Kay on the side of the road when I was driving in to the PD on Friday night. The hood of her patrol car was up and she was standing there with that big old flashlight, looking at the engine like she was ready to burn it.

"Know what the trouble is?" I asked, getting out of my car.

"No, what?" she said.

"I meant: have you figured out the problem?"

"Yeah, it won't go," she said sarcastically. "I was driving along, everything was fine, I came to the stop sign, and the car quit. Now it won't do a darned thing."

I had her get in and try the engine. Nothing. "Okay, let me get the cables out of my trunk. I'll give you a jump."

Once we had the car running, I thought I'd follow Kay to Eloise's for a bite, but the next stop sign did us in. "It's the alternator," I told her. "Didn't you notice the red light on the dash?"

"*What* red light?" she snapped. "I haven't had dash lights in two months."

I sighed. "Okay. You'll have to use your own car. Fill up the gas tank from the PD pump and make sure you put in for mileage and such. You'll have to use the walkie-talkie for communication."

"Which walkie-talkie?" she asked. "The one that works, or the one that doesn't?"

I'd forgotten that we didn't have a complete set. "I don't suppose you have a CB radio. Maybe we could—"

"Nope," she said. "You'll just have to trust me to do my job without backup."

"It's not your job I'm worried about," I told her. "It's saving your butt in a dangerous situation."

I offered her a lift to Eloise's and then home, deciding to leave Car 7 on the side of the road until the next morning. I knew Mr. Proctor wouldn't appreciate being called out to tow it at that late hour.

Handing a menu across the table to Kay, I said, "Order quick, before Eloise shuts down the grill."

Kay made a face when I ordered a cheeseburger—"That's your breakfast, Reb?"—but she was busting to tell me what she'd been up to all evening, so I didn't have to listen to the full lecture on nutrition.

"I talked to James Barrow. Boy, his wife's an iceberg, isn't she? I mean, real polite and all, but still. She tells him I'm there, and just walks away. Not a bit concerned that her husband is being questioned by the police."

"Maybe she's sure of his complete innocence."

"Come on, Reb. I think she was probably behind the door, listening. Everybody gets nervous around us. Except Wayne, of course. He's not intimidated by anybody."

"Well, Wayne's an exceptional human being," I

said, meaning it to be smart, but Kay just nodded in smug agreement. "What did you learn from Barrow?"

"He knew the Gentrys, he says, but not very well. Thought they were nice people, good neighbors. Doesn't know what time Steve Gentry came home Wednesday night. Hasn't got a clue why anyone would want to hurt Patrice."

"So talking to him was a waste of your time, then."

"I'm not so sure about that." Kay reared back in her chair and might as well have crowed. "I ran him through the computer."

"And?" I prompted.

"He's had a few speeding tickets."

"So he's never been convicted of mass murder. Too bad."

"Plus." Kay grinned.

"Is there a story in here?"

"Resisting arrest."

"For speeding?" I couldn't believe the man would worry that much about his insurance premiums being raised.

"Speeding, DUI, *then* resisting arrest. Way down in Carroll County. Guess who made his bail?"

"I give. Who?"

"Patrice Gentry."

Now, that got my attention. "He didn't know her very well, he says, but well enough that she made bail for him. What's his explanation for that?"

Kay looked properly embarrassed. "I was on my way to question him again when the car died."

"No problem. I'll swing by in the morning before he leaves for work."

"Reb," she said, "I hope you won't take this the wrong way. But you're a little bossy sometimes. You take over. You sent me to question Barrow. Now let me finish the job."

I started to argue with her, but truth is, she had a good point. And if I didn't quite trust her to get Barrow backed down until he'd tell her the whole story, well, I could always talk to him later.

"You're right, Kay," I said. "You go back and talk to him. See what you can get out of him."

That perked her right up, and she tore into her dinner like a hungry bear. I had to admit, she'd done good. Checking the computer was a nitpicky thing to do, especially since James Barrow wasn't a suspect in this case. Every now and then it pays to have a hotshot rookie around.

Between bites, she told me about her evening's work. "I spent an hour helping German decide which kind of birdseed to use. They don't want anyone throwing rice at the wedding, but they can't choose between millet and sunflower seed. I think Delia's been talking to them."

"Figures. Why the hell doesn't he let Pam do it, then? With her knack for organization, she could nail this wedding in an hour's time."

"Because it's his wedding, too, and he wants to be part of the planning." Kay had that look in her eyes, the one that tells me she's probably got poor old Wayne's tux on layaway.

"Aside from planning this wedding, did we do anything today?"

She pulled a notebook from her front pocket. "I spent over an hour at the nursing home, talking to the afternoon shift. They haven't replaced Patrice Gentry yet, so the other charge nurses are working extra shifts and they're a mite irritable. But the residents were helpful."

"Were they, now?" I asked skeptically. "What'd they do? Drool on demand?"

"You know, Reb," she said, sounding too much like my mother for comfort, "a great many of those people are completely fine. They just can't, or don't, want to live alone anymore, so they've gone to the nursing home. Miss Laura Porter, for instance, seems to have been close to Patrice. Miss Laura was a nurse herself, until her retirement, and she said Patrice was a credit to her cap. In fact, Miss Laura says Patrice was the most skilled and compassionate woman she'd ever met."

"Does Miss Laura say why someone might have killed Patrice?"

Kay shook her head. "She couldn't imagine. In fact, Ned Richardson and Virginia Steele—both of whom I'd adopt in a minute, by the way—agree. They've all three been in the home for years and known Patrice ever since she came to work there."

"And did any of these folks tell you something about Patrice Gentry that might prove *useful*?"

"Sorry, no. Their rooms all look out over the far side of the nursing home, away from the parking lot."

"What about patients with rooms that do face the parking lot? Did you talk to them?"

Kay just shook her head. "Those rooms are re-

served for the residents who aren't quite . . . aware.
The noise of cars starting up and driving through
doesn't bother them so much."

"Damn," I said.

"Except for one who requested that she be put on
that side because she likes to know who's coming
and going."

"Now, that's what I want to hear. Who is this patient, and did you get anything out of her?"

"It's Constance Winter," Kay said. "I got a lot of
information from her, but you aren't going to like
it."

"I'm sure you're right."

"To begin with, I think she's been hanging out
with Henry Mooten. She said one night a while
back, she looked out the window in the middle of
the night and saw a, quote, spaceman."

"Uh-huh. Get a description?"

"Space helmet, shiny space suit, not too tall."

"I'll ask Henry if that sounds like anybody he
knows."

"She also said that she saw Patrice Gentry taking a nap in her car one night. But she's not sure
when, and she can't remember *why* she thought
Patrice was napping."

Miss Constance was up and roaming the halls
when I got to the nursing home about midnight.
She pushes along in that wheelchair like Darrell
Waltrip on a good day, using just her one function-
ing arm, and you'd never know from looking at her
that she's crazy as a loon. She stopped in front of

the nurses' desk to confer with her poker buddy, Laura Simpson.

"Reb Gassler," she said when she saw me, "what in the world are you doing here?"

"Just taking care of a little business," I said. "How you doing this morning, Miss Constance? Miss Laura?"

"Fair to middlin', I reckon," replied Miss Constance. "Won a dollar and thirty-five cents last night." She held up one of those plastic, squeeze-open change purses. I didn't even know they still made those. "You here about the murder, I guess."

I was surprised that she knew anything about it. Seems like they'd keep news like that from the patients. But since she did know, I didn't see any point in pretending.

"Yes, ma'am. I've got to ask some more questions, find out if her coworkers knew anything about Mrs. Gentry that might help us catch her killer."

"Oh, Chief." Miss Laura sighed. "I certainly hope you do catch him. Poor little Patrice was just the best thing. Her heart was so full of love—" . . . and about here I lost track of the words. Miss Laura had started to cry and blubber, and her hands were dancing in the air. I couldn't tell if she was trying to find a hanky or if she was swatting at something in the air.

I reached into my back pocket and pulled out my handkerchief to give her. Miss Laura took it and covered her whole face, still shaking and heaving. Once in a while I'd catch a word, like *loved* or *generous*, but for the most part she was just babbling out her grief.

Breaks my heart to see something like that. Poor Miss Laura, so old and fragile and vulnerable, was crying like every sadness in her life had come to roost at once. Tell the truth, it caused me to tear up a little.

"Why don't I push you back to your room?" I offered, taking hold of the wheelchair. I wasn't sure whether she said yes or no, but I didn't think she'd want to sit out there in the hall, losing her dignity in front of everybody. And even if she didn't care, it made me uncomfortable as hell.

I rolled her up to the bed and pushed the call light so the nurse could come and do whatever needed doing. I sure didn't aim to undress Miss Laura and tuck her in! Then I went back out to finish the conversation with Miss Constance.

"Well, I can tell you all you need to know. That girl was a saint sent from heaven above to take care of us old folks. Don't surprise me none that she's dead, though. The world's gettin' to be a terrible place, and that there parking lot is a den of sin. I've seen what goes on out there."

"I'm sorry you've been exposed to such as that, Miss Constance," I said, thinking it would be ungentlemanly to ask for details of what she'd seen. And besides, why waste the breath when I knew what she was going to tell me anyway.

"Young hoodlums running loose. Parents don't watch their young'uns like they did in my day. Let 'em out like that, any time of the day or night. Young'uns don't have enough chores to keep 'em busy, that's the problem."

"Do you happen to know who these young'uns are?" I asked, mentally crossing my fingers.

"How can anybody tell? They're all dressed like ragamuffins, which is a sign of our deteriorating society."

Sounded to me like Miss Constance had been exposed to public television, too, since she'd been in the home.

"You go door-to-door, ask these parents where their kids are at night. Any of 'em that tell you they don't know, theirs are the hoodlums you're looking for."

"I'll surely do it, ma'am," I promised. "Uh, what sort of trouble would these young people be in if I found them?"

"Vandals!" she said. "Tearing up jack. No respect."

With that she wheeled herself away, bursting into song as she went. "R-E-S-P-E-C-T." I'll bet Aretha never thought it would be done that way.

I stood at the nurses' desk for about five minutes more before Diane Forsythe bustled by, tucking a wad of rubber gloves and a handful of disposable syringes into her uniform pocket. "Sorry, Chief," she said. "That evening shift doesn't get half the work done and then it's left for me to clean up afterward and do my work, too." She rubbed at a red stain on her uniform pocket and frowned when it remained stubbornly in place.

"Blood?" I asked.

"Ink. Midnight shift," she said enigmatically. When she saw that I was confused, she explained. "Midnight shift charts in red ink. Days in blue or black, evenings in green. That way we can tell from a glance what shift administered what treatment or med. I'm always sticking my pen in my pocket without capping it. You'd think I'd learn. But I'm running around most of the time like a chicken with its head cut off, and I forgot the little things."

"I apologize for adding to your troubles, but I need some of your time. The one thing you can't spare, huh?"

She grinned at me. "You got that right. Time and money."

"Can we grab some coffee and sit down?"

"Sure." She led me around behind the desk and poured coffee into two Styrofoam cups. "We've got sugar and creamer around here somewhere."

"No, thanks. Don't want to dilute it any. I'd just as soon inject it."

"Working midnights," she said, and nodded. "Now, what can I tell you?"

"Miss Constance was just telling me about the hoodlums in the parking lot outside."

Diane raised her eyebrows and ran a hand over her hair. "Miss Constance. Last night she told me a knight on a white horse was in her room."

"I don't suppose you found any hoofprints on the floor. But there *has* been some evidence left in the parking lot. Several cases of vandalism lately."

"Oh, yes. Tires slashed, windows broken. We don't know who's responsible, though. It always happens on my shift and I'm locked away in here, where I can't hear a thing that happens. Wish I could, though. I'd love to catch the little creeps who ruined my new tires."

"I noticed the other day that you're a smoker. They don't let you smoke in here, though, do they?"

"No, not anymore. I have to go outside. When I can find the time."

"So you've never seen anything at all suspicious when you've been out there on a smoking break?"

I thought she shivered just a little. "No. And it's never even occurred to me that someone might have been out there with me. That's frightening. Good Lord! You don't suppose I was out there when Patrice's killer . . . oh, shit."

She didn't seem terrified by the thought, but something in her changed. I couldn't put my finger on it.

"Reb, I'm sure I didn't see a thing. But is it possible there was something I didn't pay attention to? Something important?"

"Could be," I agreed. "Happens once in a while." Once in a blue moon. "Don't get tense about it, but if something does occur to you, give me a call. Or talk to one of my officers."

"I will. I promise." She finished her coffee and tossed the cup into the trash can.

"What I really wanted to get from you, though, is some information about Patrice Gentry."

"I can't help you there, Chief. I barely knew her."

"But she worked this shift sometimes, didn't she?"

Diane nodded. "If I had to be off, sometimes Patrice would fill in for me. Once or twice, when things were especially hectic—like if I had a couple of residents dying on me, for instance—Patrice would stay over to help out. We were far too busy on those nights to chat, though."

"So you don't have any idea about her personal life? People who might have held a grudge. Someone she might have ticked off?"

Diane shook her head. "Sorry, Chief."

"And when you took over from her that night, she seemed fine?"

"Absolutely. She gave report just like always and went home. At least, she left."

"What about your aides on this shift? I need to talk to them."

"I'll round them up for you. And then I've got to get the meds out. Sorry I haven't been more help."

"You may have been more help than you know." That's a little parting shot I like to use. Keeps people on their toes, never knowing what they might have said to me.

The aides were a couple of skinny little girls, barely out of their teens, who didn't look like they could lift a bedridden patient if their lives depended on it. *They* were eager to talk to me, but mostly about the actual murder—cause of death, how bloody was it, all the gory details. For all their interest, they didn't know a thing about Patrice Gentry. Probably couldn't have picked her out of a crowd of two.

I left there feeling like the best information I'd gotten had come from Miss Constance. Stepping through the door to the outside was like crossing the border between life and the grave. Inside the home, there'd been a musty, dead smell. The gallons of antibacterial cleansers couldn't make the place smell like anything other than rotting flesh and moldering dreams.

The stagnant air muffled noise, too, shutting out the world as if to guard against any suggestion of hope. The only sounds inside that building were the moans of agony and despair.

Out in the open, I took a deep breath and filled my lungs with free-moving oxygen, trying not to think about the inevitable day when I'd be trapped inside with no chance of escape.

CHAPTER

5

Love and comfort

MY CAR IS QUIETER THAN THAT PATROL car, so I expect the local residents slept right through my shift. Could have done that, myself. The one time I'm keyed up and ready for action is the night all the felons and drunks decided to stay off the streets. Go figure that one.

I took a swing by your house, by the way, and all was quiet. Too quiet. The house looks sad and empty when you're not there. Like me.

Sure could have used something to occupy my mind right then, and patrolling Jesus Creek isn't a brain stretcher. Lately I've been careful to circle all the parking lots, especially the dark ones. Out at the nursing home they've replaced one of the busted-out security lights. Maybe if they'd done that sooner . . . I thought, but I knew it was pointless. Whatever happened to cause Patrice Gentry's death wouldn't have been changed by a light. Something that big gets to rolling, nothing's gonna stop it.

With no new crime to investigate, I went looking for sleaze instead. My first pass in front of Amanda Brewer's house was about two A.M. She's got a bumper sticker that says SAVE THE WHALES, and every time I've seen her, she's been wearing a red ribbon. But would you believe there's a sign in her front yard that urges us to PROTECT OUR NATIVE PLANTS? She lives out on the highway in one of those little square rental houses. Hers is the one with blue shutters.

For a renter, she's fixed the place up real nice. Tulips in the window boxes, and a birdbath in the front yard with some kind of flowers around it. The ones with black in the middle. What do you call those?

And sure enough, Gentry's car was parked in the driveway and there wasn't a light on anywhere. Taking comfort in the other woman's arms the night before his wife's memorial service. Charming man.

I knew it would be Monday at least before we could get Gentry's financial records, but I was willing to bet we'd find his wife's life had been insured for big bucks, and that he was about to inherit every dime. I wanted this guy.

Still thinking of ways to make Gentry suffer, I drove past the Veatch house, but all was quiet there, too. I couldn't even find any teenagers cruising, so I drove down to the courthouse and backed the car into one of the parking spaces there. I'd forgotten to take my pillow out of the patrol car, so I had to settle for leaning my head back on the seat.

It was a damned peculiar case. I had a dead woman with no enemies. I also had a good suspect with two alibis, neither of which matched what he'd told me himself, or with what Anne Barrow had said. Could *she* have a reason for lying about Gentry coming in around midnight? I'd have to ponder that for a while.

I had a town full of folks who'd swear Gentry loved his wife. What was it with these Gentrys? I wondered. How did they inspire such loyalty and devotion in near strangers?

And on the next page, I had a string of break-ins that made no sense whatsoever. When the stolen items are radios and silver, I understand. Who takes radios and silver and wheat bread and blankets? Somebody setting up housekeeping? Somebody looking for inexpensive ways to do their Christmas shopping?

Which led me to think about a wedding gift for German and Pam. I don't suppose I could persuade you to pick one out for me? I never know what newlyweds need. And besides, they've both got houses full of junk. Maybe I should just stick a check in an envelope and give them that.

For the life of me, I don't understand why Pam and German want to get married. Can't they just keep their separate homes and commute from one bed to the other? You don't suppose they're planning to have kids? Good Lord, I hadn't thought of that.

No, I don't reckon it's got a damned thing to do with love. Even if it has, Pam ought to have better sense. I can tell that German's got his head in the clouds, but you'd think *she* would have considered the possibilities. Find me a marriage that hasn't ended in divorce, and I'll show you a marriage that ought to have ended in divorce.

Animal instinct leads to breeding, yeah. But the way it all looks to me, animal instinct tells us to make each other's lives just as miserable as we can. Marriage is just a means to that end. You can do a lot more damage to the other person when you're legally bound. But you know that, don't you?

I finally dozed off a few minutes before sunrise—just enough sleep to leave my mouth furry and my mood foul. I was sorry about that until I remembered that I was going to talk to Gentry. I *wanted* to be in a nasty mood when I talked to him.

Just for the fun of it, I decided not to wait for him at his house. I went to Amanda Brewer's instead and pounded on her front door until she answered it. She's a right fetching sight first thing in the morning. All that dark hair tumbled over her face, like the women on the covers of those romance novels. She probably dressed up for company, because I don't think she'd ordinarily wander around her own house in a green silk robe. Particularly not one that short, what with the weather still being reasonably cool in the early morning.

"Morning, Miss Brewer," I said, with a big grin on my face. "I'm here to talk to Dr. Gentry. Is he up?" Tacky of me, wasn't it?

She was shaking her head, getting ready to deny that he was up, or there, or able to talk, or something, when he came out of the bedroom dressed in jeans and a sweatshirt. His hair was tousled, but in such a way as to look like a Hollywood hairdresser had run his hands through it. Morning beard stubble, which makes me look like a reeling drunk, gave Gentry an air of casual sophistication. I sure hoped he'd spent an hour getting to look like that. There's nothing I despise more than a man who looks good when he first crawls out of bed.

"Chief Gassler," he said, without a hint of shame. "Please come in. Is there a problem?"

If his wife being murdered wasn't problem enough for him, then he'd lost me.

"Nothing new," I said. "But I'd like to talk to you. Sorry to have to do this on the day of your wife's service." I hoped they both caught that. When Gentry at least should have been getting ready to attend the memorial service for his murdered wife, he was lounging in the home and bed of his mistress.

"I understand," Gentry told me. "Why don't we have a seat here while Amanda makes us some coffee?"

Amanda obediently headed for the kitchen while Gentry made himself comfortable in the love seat and motioned for me to take the chair. From the way they acted toward each other, you'd have thought they'd been married for years.

The house was real nice on the inside, too. Oh, the furniture was cheap, but she'd taken care of it. Lots of blue and pink, which you'd think would make Gentry gag every time he walked in, but he looked right comfortable. Amanda had framed wildlife posters on the walls, along with an enlarged shot of a pitiful-looking child—the kind you see in those Christian Children Fund or Save the Children ads. I figured our Miss Brewer must have sponsored this child, which was a point in her fa-

vor. After all, she couldn't be making enough
money that she had it to spare, so being a foster
parent and shelling out her hard-earned dollars every month must have been a sacrifice.

The Amnesty International newsletter was on
her coffee table, and I could see where she'd
marked one paragraph with a red felt-tipped pen.
All in all, a woman concerned with the fate of the
world, I'd say. I couldn't help but get a little mel-
low toward her. Most people worry about it and go
on. At least Amanda was making some effort, it
seemed.

"Now, Dr. Gentry," I began, "let's start with a few
matters you may have forgotten to tell me before.
Can you think of any incident your wife mentioned
recently that might have involved trouble for her?
Someone who'd given her a hard time at work, or
at the grocery store? Anywhere?"

"Absolutely not," he assured me. "Patrice was a
sweet, gentle soul. Everyone adored her." His voice
sort of broke right there and he sniffed a little. "I've
known her for ten years. You know, the first time I
saw her, she was running down the hall beside a
gurney, carrying an IV bottle in one hand and
stroking the patient's forehead with the other.
Compassionate is a word invented to describe
Patrice."

He had to pause to search his pockets for a han-
kie and get himself back together, but he went on
then, talking about his beloved wife. "We've worked
together in remote villages where no one had ever
heard of immunization or even simple hygiene.
Patrice would take those tiny, undernourished in-

fants in her arms, never noticing the open sores or
flies that swarmed around them, and give them so
much love you'd have thought she'd run out. But
she never did."

He'd gotten lost in his memories, sitting there re-
living the precious moments while his mistress
made coffee. Touching.

I wondered if Amanda had heard any of what
he'd said. Wouldn't you think she'd have been
steaming? I mean, hell. The guy's sleeping with her
and going on and on about his wife. Of course, this
made me more certain than ever that he was guilty
of Patrice's murder. He had to be putting on a show
for me.

When Amanda rejoined us, Gentry was talking
about the way Patrice worried about her patients
at the nursing home—their fear and loneliness. He
said she'd bought Christmas presents for all of
them, and how she remembered each and every
one's birthday with a little gift.

"Oh, that's right," Amanda chimed in. "She gave
Miss Constance a new set of poker chips. I remember Patrice worried about how to wrap them, because, you know, Miss Constance only has that one
good arm and Patrice wasn't sure she'd be able to
get past the tape and paper. She finally stitched up
a drawstring bag, and Miss Constance just loved
it!"

Get this. The husband and the other woman
were sharing happy memories of the wife. I wanted
to throw up.

"Everybody has enemies," I pointed out.

"Not Patrice," Gentry and Amanda said together,

then looked at each other and giggled like teenagers who had just discovered they both like the same music.

Time to move on, I thought. "So, Dr. Gentry. You said your wife often worked an extra shift, and you didn't find anything unusual about her not coming home on time the night she was murdered."

He had the decency to flinch at that, but he shook his head. "Not at all."

"And you went to bed at what time that night?"

Before Gentry could answer, Amanda jumped in. "He was here with me all night, Chief."

For a split second I saw confusion in Gentry's eyes, but then he answered. "Oh, yes. I'd forgotten. I suppose the shock, you know. I believe I told you earlier that I'd been at home, but in fact, I was here. With Amanda."

"All night," I repeated.

"Yes, that's correct."

"So, had your wife come home on time, you wouldn't have been there anyway?"

"No, I wouldn't have been there." Gentry sighed.

"And your wife wouldn't have found anything odd about that?"

Gentry seemed at a loss, but Amanda quickly rescued him. "He's often called in for an emergency during the night, Chief. Patrice would have assumed that had happened."

I felt as if I'd been picked up and dumped right smack dab in the middle of a *Geraldo* segment. If there had been even a little bit of embarrassment from those two, even a hint of remorse . . . but they were sitting there talking about how they duped his wife the way they'd explain a recipe.

"Your neighbors claim they heard you come home that night around midnight. That would have been just after your wife was murdered. How do you explain that?"

Gentry was floundering around for an answer, so obliging Amanda jumped in and saved him. "They're mistaken," she said firmly. She looked me right in the eye, calm as could be. "He was with me all that night."

The girl was either an expert liar, or she was telling the total truth. I honestly didn't know which, and that made me uncomfortable. I don't like not knowing. Besides, that had been my trump card and now that I'd played it, I realized I didn't have much of a hand left. I figured I'd better move on quick, before Gentry realized I was in trouble.

"And your wife didn't have a clue about you—ah, having an affair with Miss Brewer here?"

"Oh, of course not," Gentry said. "I'd never hurt her like that. Patrice would have been devastated. Amanda and I have taken great care to be discreet."

Proud of themselves, they were. "I see," I said. Finally I got a minute's satisfaction when I added, "And what about your affair with Teresa Simmons? Are you as discreet about that?"

Amanda's mouth dropped open.

I tell you, I enjoyed that. When I left Amanda Brewer's house, there was a big old grin on my face and my heart felt light and happy. I went in to

Eloise's Diner feeling almost as good as if I'd solved
the case.

Henry and his election committee were slurping
up biscuits and gravy at the center table, and Delia
was with Roger in the corner. I decided to join Delia and Roger before the others spotted me, and
just hollered out my sausage-and-egg order to
Eloise.

"What is this?" Delia asked. "Cholesterol Cen-
tral?"

I noted that she was having a bran muffin and
fruit. Roger (who isn't nearly as bad a guy as I'd
first thought) was chowing down on pancakes
loaded with butter and syrup.

"I heard that bran causes brain tumors," I told
her.

"Behave, or we'll make you sit with Henry." Delia
glanced over at the other table. "Although I plan to
vote for him. He has a brilliant campaign slogan:
*For simple values and simpler times, vote for a sim-
ple man.*"

"That pretty well sums it up," I agreed.

"Roger thought of it," Delia pointed out. And
Roger snickered.

"Trying to get back in the town's good graces after all the stunts you've pulled?" I asked.

"I'm trying to help my candidate win," Roger
said. "It seemed like a slogan that Jesus Creek residents would appreciate."

"Well, that's just great, Roger," I said. "Now
you've given a helping hand to the man who wants
to make Jesus Creek home to the Martians."

"You don't think they've taken over already?" he asked.

Delia interrupted us to ask about the Gentry case. "Any new clues? I hope so, because this is one person I want thrown in prison for life."

"Nothing worth mentioning," I said. "But I'm curious about something. Back when you were teaching, Delia, did you ever know a kid named Amanda Brewer? She looks young enough to have been one of your students."

"Not one of my *students*," Delia said. "But she was a teacher's helper. The high-schoolers who joined Future Teachers of America would come over to the elementary and junior high schools one day a week to help in the classroom. I had Amanda one year. Why are you interested in her?"

"She's Gentry's nurse, down at his office."

"Yes," Delia said. "That doesn't tell me why you're interested."

"You've surely heard—"

"That she's been having an affair with Dr. Gentry. Heard it. So what's your point?"

"So she's given the man an alibi. That makes her a player. How far would you believe her?"

Delia shrugged. "Amanda is a kindhearted girl. I remember there was a big stink in her science class when she refused to dissect a frog. Took a failing grade for the term rather than give in. When she helped out in my classroom, I often set her to work with individual pupils who needed extra attention. She was wonderful with them, by the way, and it's a shame she decided to go into nursing instead of education, although I suppose medicine offers a more hands-on approach to helping others."

"But is she trustworthy?" I asked.

"She's an animal-rights activist. She's patient and loving and bright and she's trying as hard as she can to make the world a better place for us all. How can you *not* trust someone like that?"

"Sounds like another Patrice Gentry to me," I said. Just what I needed. Maybe Gentry had a type, but I doubted Teresa Simmons was it. Maybe Teresa was the liar. Surely Gentry was. Possibly, if improbably, Amanda was.

I had the feeling that if I could just figure out the puzzle of which *one* person was telling the truth, all the other pieces would fall into place.

Eloise brought out my coffee and breakfast and gave me a shoulder punch. "By Jesus, Reb. You've stirred up a hornet's nest," she said.

"Who, me?"

"Yes, you. Here we've all been thinking that Dr. Gentry is the best thing since chocolate. Then you came in here, asking about him running around with women. So I did some checking."

"You didn't believe me when I told you?"

"Sure, I *believed* you. But I needed more details. Come to find out, that man's slept with half the women in this town."

I put the coffee cup on the table and pulled out my notepad. "Names, please," I said.

It took two pages to write them all down.

CHAPTER

6

Honor and keep

SUNDAY HAS ITS OWN SPECIAL FEEL, YOU
know? I could wake up from a ten-year sleep and
know whether or not it's Sunday, just by the air
around me.

I thought there might be something sacrilegious
about questioning Gentry's women on a Sunday,
but I woke up that afternoon full of energy, ready
to get moving. The sun was out and people were
bustling around, doing nothing in particular but
happy to have spring back again. I knew how they
felt. Just a week before, I'd thought I'd never see
green again, and suddenly the trees and yards had
busted out like they'd been shot full of steroids.

I found Kay down on Morning Glory, sitting on
the hood of her patrol car, pretending to write up a
report. Actually she was working on her tan. I
pulled up beside her car and hopped up there with
her, even though I saw no point in sunbathing, myself.

"Enjoying your shift?" I asked her.

Without a trace of embarrassment, she said,
"Yep. Ever thought about uniforms with shorts?
And tank tops? I could get an even tan that way."

"I asked for a bikini just for you, but the mayor wanted to know where you'd pin the badge, and for the life of me, I couldn't come up with an answer."

"Hey, I deserve this," she insisted. "I've done exemplary work this afternoon. I talked to the day-shift nurses at the Home for the Terminally Aged and I did *this*. The James Barrow report."

"Nurses know anything?"

"Oh, yes," she said. "They know all about bed-pans and needles and medications. But they don't know a blessed thing about Patrice Gentry."

"Figures."

"In fact, the whole shift was on a scavenger hunt for four-by-four pads. Seems they've misplaced a box of said pads and I gather that's a serious sin. James Barrow was more interesting." She held out the report she'd been working on.

I ignored the written report in favor of what was sure to be a more animated verbal rendition from Officer Kay. "What's his explanation?"

"For the bail? Well, first he tried to tell me I was mistaken—that he'd never been arrested in his life, that he'd never met Patrice Gentry, and that now that he thought about it, he wasn't even James Barrow. Needless to say, I told him he was wrong."

"Needless to say," I agreed. Kay takes great joy in coming out on top, so I didn't doubt she'd enjoyed playing bad cop with James Barrow. If he hadn't been so stupid, I'd have felt sorry for the guy.

"And then, when I'd convinced him I knew every secret detail of his life, he proceeded to blab way more than I ever wanted to know." She leaned back on the windshield and hooked her thumbs through imaginary suspenders, a look of sheer pride on her face.

"Feel free to leave out the unimportant details," I encouraged her.

"Admission from Mr. Barrow: he was, indeed, stopped for DUI, and did, at the time, possess a small quantity of cocaine. This caused him great concern, as he believed he might be arrested for breaking some law about which he professed total ignorance. The officer did not believe him."

"And they say cops are dumb," I muttered.

"When the officer made clear his intention of doing his duty—that is, to arrest Mr. Barrow—the situation turned ugly."

I waved at Delia and Roger, who were strolling the block, and returned to Kay's fascinating tale. "How ugly?"

"Barrow busted the cop's nose," she said.

"Must not have been too drunk if he could aim that well," I pointed out.

"The cop says it was a lucky punch. Otherwise he agrees with everything Mr. Barrow told me."

"Are we getting to the part that interests me?" I asked, slightly impatient.

Kay stuck her tongue in her cheek and made that clicking noise that my mother used to give me when she thought I was pushing too fast. "Barrow was taken in and allowed his phone call. He says he didn't dare call his wife, as she would have raised holy hell. He obviously didn't have bail money on him—well, one assumes he'd just spent it on booze and goodness knows what else—so he wasn't sure what to do. Then he remembered the new neighbors."

"Always my first thought when I'm in trouble. Call a stranger for help. A lawyer would never occur to me."

Kay nodded solemnly. "I told you Barrow is stupid."

"What interests me more, though, is Patrice Gentry running to his side. You don't suppose she was more than a passing acquaintance?"

"Occurred to me," Kay said. "Why should Gentry be the only one fudging on his vows? Barrow says not, though. He says he'd talked to Patrice a few times, knew she was a nice lady, and trusted her to keep quiet."

I wondered how Barrow had come to his conclusions if he'd merely met Patrice a few times. It didn't sound convincing, but it was a start. "I say we keep an eye on Barrow. Would it offend your honor if I talked to him?"

"Not if you admit that I was brilliant to think of this in the first place."

"You can have it in writing. I wonder if Barrow paid her back."

"Says he did," Kay muttered. The sunshine was making her sleepy, but it had the opposite effect on me.

"Get back in your car," I told her. "Drive around for a while, or at least get some coffee." I slid off the hood and headed for my own car. "I'm going over to harass Barrow."

"Enjoy," Kay said without opening her eyes.

Sleepy little town we've got here. Cops doze away

their time on duty, neighborhood watch is the order of the day, and the folks next door are real good to make bail for strangers. Just like Mayberry. If you don't count the dead bodies.

James Barrow was just pulling into his driveway when I got there. He had a couple of kids bouncing around in the backseat and I felt sure they'd never been in the seat belts to start with. The kids tumbled out of the car together and I noticed that one had catsup smeared across its face. From this I deduced that Dad had taken them out for quickie burgers somewhere.

"Afternoon, Mr. Barrow," I said, in that congenial fashion you know so well.

"Chief," he replied. He may have been nervous, or maybe I just thought he ought to be. Either way, he waited for me to continue.

"Officer Martin tells me she spoke to you earlier. Could I ask you to clarify a few things for me?"

"I thought I'd explained that already. What's left to cover?"

You'll notice he didn't invite me in. No doubt because the rug rats had already bounded through the front door and turned the television on so loud I could hear it in the yard.

"About this bail that Miz Gentry made for you," I began, "after you were arrested for assaulting an officer, possession of illegal substances, and driving under the influence of alcohol—" I listed the crimes in case he'd forgotten, or in case he thought I wasn't fully aware of what a miscreant he was. "I was just wondering. Usually folks will get a family

member or a least a real good friend to post their
bail. But you called a neighbor you barely knew.
Now, why is that, Mr. Barrow?"

I was happy to see him squirm. Apparently he'd
never considered this. Finally, with sweat starting
to form on his forehead (and it wasn't that hot outside), he stuttered, "Well ... ah ... I don't have
family in this area."

"Your wife, Mr. Barrow? You might have called
her that night."

"Look, Chief. You don't know my wife. She'd have
been on my back forever. She still doesn't know
about what happened and I hope you'll keep it
quiet."

"Don't you think she's likely to hear about your
arrest at some point? When it goes to court, for instance?"

A crease popped in between his eyes. Obviously
worried. "No, no," he said after a bit. "The court
date is for midday. I'll leave for work like always.
She'll never have to know."

Now I'm standing there listening to him plan
how to outsmart his wife when he goes to court. I'm
in uniform, I've got the badge and the gun, and he's
working out the details in front of me. Is it just me,
or is this guy a nitwit?

"Well, let's say you're convicted. Think she might
notice that?"

Sheer, uncontrolled terror took hold of the man.
"Convicted? I hadn't thought—"

What? I wondered. Hadn't thought he'd be convicted? Hadn't thought the little woman might notice his absence? Suddenly I could believe he'd

really called a near stranger to bail him out of jail. It's a wonder he didn't call *me*.

I left him standing there in his front yard, probably contemplating the cruel reality facing him. Poor guy hadn't once considered the possibility that he'd be convicted, and I wondered why not. Was he thoroughly stupid? Wildly cocky? It was no wonder that Anne Barrow was such an iceberg. Somebody in that family had to be in control, and it sure as hell wouldn't have been him.

Next on my list of fun activities was questioning all those women Eloise had found out about. Of course, looking at the names on the list, what I really wanted to know was this: what vitamin is Gentry taking?

I started at the top of the list, with Sandy Melton. I'm pretty sure you know her. She worked part-time for Eloise a while back, and now she's working at that factory in Benton Harbor. She's divorced again and living in a trailer off the highway, out west of town.

She invited me right in, like I was the last guest at a party and they'd been waiting dinner on me. "Reb, you stinker!" she said, when she'd put me at the kitchen table and poured a glass of tea for me. "Where have you been lately? I hadn't seen you in ages."

I'd taken a look at the place while she was fussing with the tea, and I gotta tell you, it didn't look like anywhere Gentry would have been comfortable. This is an old trailer we're talking about here. Stuffing coming out of the couch, garbage piled up by the kitchen sink, and curtains so dirty and limp I couldn't even tell what color they were supposed to be.

"Now, Sandy," I said, trying not to touch the surface of the table, "you know what a busy man I am. I move like a snake, slithering here and there, surprising wrongdoers."

"Shit you do," she said, pushing a lock of hair out of her face. "You sleep your life away down behind the Drink Tank. You're too old to sleep in a car, Reb. If you're gonna get a crick in your neck, it ought to be from something more exciting than sleeping."

"I'm too old for that, too," I admitted. "Although I hear you're as young as ever. Steve Gentry?"

"Poor old Steve," she said, and sighed. "Losing his wife like that. It's just awful is what it is. Who'd want to kill a woman like that?"

"Got any guesses?"

"I wish I did," she said fervently. "Poor Steve was crazy in love with that woman, and from all I hear, she felt the same way about him. It's terrible the way the world's going."

"Excuse me," I said, "but from what I've heard, you were a good bit closer to Steve Gentry than to his wife."

Sandy whipped out an evil grin. "Close don't begin to describe it," she said, without shame.

"So how long has this romance been going on?" I asked.

"Romance! That's a good one. You ever get a purely physical urge, Reb?" she asked, and tried to bat her lashes at me.

"So what? You don't care a hoot for Gentry except in a physical sense?"

"I think the world of the man," she insisted. "But romance is hardly what I'd call it. Wild and hairy sex, now that's a perfect description. And if he happens to be a decent, caring man, am I gonna complain?"

Much as I would have liked hearing the details, I decided it might be more than my heart could stand. "You know, then, that several other women were having sex or romance or whatever you'd call it with Steve Gentry?"

"Well, talent like that shouldn't go to waste," she said flatly.

"I expect his wife wouldn't have minded if he'd kept it at home," I pointed out.

"Hey, he's a cool guy. He kept it quiet. Well, as quiet as you can keep anything around here. And he really, truly loved that woman. What did she have to complain about?"

I left Sandy's place still confused and fuming. How come nobody but me considered Gentry's dallying disgraceful? Didn't any of these women want a loyal man? They all seemed to know about the others. Well, maybe Amanda hadn't, but even after I made her aware of the situation, she kept right on seeing Gentry.

Most of what I'd been wondering came right out my mouth when I met Annette Gibson. She's been in Jesus Creek for years, she told me. I guess I must have seen her around, but she doesn't hang out at the diner and she's never been in trouble with the law, so I never paid attention.

She was trimming the grass around the edge of her sidewalk when I arrived and explained why I was there.

"Have a seat," she said, real friendly, and pointed to the porch swing.

She was wearing jeans and an old shirt, but I could tell from her haircut and her neat hands that she was a classy number. Not harsh, like Anne Barrow, but genuinely well-bred, with a soft, easy manner that made me want to shake her hard until she realized what a fool she'd been to take up with Gentry.

"Explain it to me, please," I said. "All you women flock around him like he's the best thing since God. And he's sleeping with half the town even though he says he loves his wife. I just don't get it."

Annette smiled, like she could fully understand my confusion. "Steve is an attractive man," she pointed out. Unnecessarily. "He's also kind and compassionate, intelligent, witty. But most of all, he truly loves women. In general."

"Yeah, I noticed," I said.

That got a little laugh out of her. "That wasn't exactly what I meant. Steve loves the species. He *appreciates* women, and most men don't. A man who goes out of his way to make a woman feel special is worth the trouble."

"Worth sneaking around? And having your reputation ruined?"

"Well, a reputation isn't something that matters so much anymore," she said. "And Steve is discreet. Besides, Chief, there's something to be said for the excitement of secret passion."

I rocked back and forth in the swing a few times, remembering my youthful encounters in the backseat of a '55 Chevy. "That explains—but not very well—why a nice woman like you would get involved with Gentry. But what about his claims that he loved his wife? Hell, why didn't he just divorce her and make himself free to run around with all the women he could find?"

"He doesn't just love his wife," she pointed out. "He adores her. He worships her. She is the brightest spot in his life and always will be. But you see, Chief," she said, leaning forward like she was about to explain the mysteries of the universe, "he loves change, too. The unexpected, the new, the excitement of romance. He needs all that to make his life complete. Unfortunately, now that Patrice is dead, he's lost part of himself that he'll never be able to replace. It's terribly sad, isn't it?"

Her eyes welled up with tears and I decided I'd better leave. Life was starting to feel like a *Twilight Zone* episode.

Seven more women from the list Eloise had given me seemed to agree with Sandy. Oh, some of them had nicer houses and some had better grammar, and some were a whole lot worse looking than Sandy will ever be, but in general, they adored Steve Gentry. He'd talked to every single one of them about his wife and how much he loved her. Yet nobody thought there was anything peculiar about his affairs.

Two of these women, mind you, claimed to be wildly in love with the doctor. Some of them considered themselves participants in a long-term serious

relationship with him. Some saw him once in a
great while. But every doggoned one of them spoke
highly of the man.

Sometimes I wonder what became of the world
when I wasn't looking.

Patrice Gentry's memorial service was set for
that afternoon. I'd avoided it on principle. You
know I hate funerals, even when the body isn't
there. But I did park outside the church and note
the number of cars. Lots.

And in spite of the request in Patrice's will that
donations be made to St. Jude's, quite a few people
had sent flowers. I watched the florist carry them
in, then I watched her carry them out again after
the service. I imagine they'd have been taken to the
hospital patients afterward.

I recognized most of the mourners—nurses, hospital staff, several folks from around town who'd
probably been patients of Dr. Gentry's at some
point. I thought it was odd that James and Anne
Barrow weren't there, though.

Gentry left the church on the arm of Amanda
Brewer, but several other women were hovering at
his side. Amanda pretended not to notice the com-
petition.

I waited until the last mourner had left before
pulling out and heading for Eloise's. Thought I'd
have a hearty meal then go home and try to catch
a few hours' sleep before my shift. I was just finish-
ing my pie when I saw Kay whiz by the diner at
breakneck speed.

Expecting the worst, I borrowed Eloise's phone to

call Al at the PD. "Something up, buddy?" I asked him. "Kay just went tearing down the street—"

"If you're awake, Chief, you'd better give her a hand. Four different people have called in already. Somebody went through town today and ripped off houses one right after another."

CHAPTER

7

So long as you both shall live

PRIMROSE AVENUE LOOKED LIKE THERE
was a block party in progress. Kay's car was sur-
rounded by irate citizens, while other, less outraged
residents of the street roamed from yard to yard ex-
changing stories.

Kay caught sight of me and almost fainted with
relief. "Reb!" she called. "Get over here and start
taking notes."

"Don't tell them you were sunning yourself while
their houses were being broken into," I whispered
to her. Then to the crowd I said, "Please line up in
an orderly fashion and we'll take your statements."

It was the strangest damned sight you ever saw.
A dozen or more people, all decked out in their funeral finery, practically fighting to be first to tell
the story. They all crowded around me at once,
leaving Kay looking a little put out because they'd
ignored her. Times haven't changed so much that
the average citizen doesn't still trust a hale-and-
hearty *male* officer more than a sweet little female.
Or even Kay.

It took a little while, but we managed to get two
lines going. All the stories were the same. The vic-

tims had attended the memorial service for Patrice
Gentry, then returned home to find they'd been
burgled. The stolen items were just as odd an as-
sortment as any. Mrs. Arwood was missing a VCR,
two forks, a tablespoon, and one knife from her
Buttercup, not to mention a place setting of the
good Melmac. The Knotts lost only a VCR and a set
of chartreuse-and-orange towels and a bar of soap.
The Marks family had been robbed of their new
computer and their prized gold coin collection,
which, they told me, was worth several thousand
dollars although they had no documentation or
proof that the collection even existed. The Law-
rences said their portable phone had been stolen,
but they admitted that they never used it anymore
anyway.

On the more likely side, the Browns were missing a VCR and a twelve-gauge pump shotgun. "It's
left-handed," Mr. Brown informed me. "I had to
special-order the danged thing!" Oh, yes. And a jar
of peanut butter. Chunky.

One thing I was fairly sure of—there'd be no serial number on anything but the gun, the computer,
and VCRs.

As quickly as we could, we took names and made
promises and got the heck out of there. I instructed
Kay to meet me at Eloise's, where I hoped we'd be
able to make sense of the notes we'd taken. With
everybody talking at once like that, I doubted we'd
even written down the reason we'd been called out.

Eloise offered us coffee on the house and peered
over our shoulders while Kay and I confabbed.
"This shotgun," Kay said, "worries me. The nine-

millimeter taken from the Sikeses' house was bad enough. Now we're talking not only firepower, but *big* firepower."

"It's the peanut butter that worries me," I admitted. "Everybody knows chunky makes you mean."

"You aren't taking this seriously, Reb," Kay chided.

"I am. I'm tickled to death. The thief took a left-handed shotgun. Either he's left-handed, or he's soon gonna be sprouting a facial scar."

"Suppose he just pawns it?"

"Don't spoil my good mood, woman," I warned.

"You know what I think?" Eloise said. "I think it's kids playing around. Who else would take all that silly stuff?"

"A clever thief who hopes to throw us off the trail," I said hopefully.

"Or a lunatic," Kay pointed out.

I figured she was closer to the mark than any of us.

I crawled in to work Monday night, wishing I could have been anywhere else in the world. Car 7 was still out of commission and Mr. Proctor said it would stay that way until somebody bought it a new alternator. I found Kay pulled to the side of the road in front of the school, kicking a flat tire on Car 12.

"You're mighty rough on cars, Kay," I told her.

"The damage was done long before I came along," she snapped back. "These old junkers aren't safe. When are you going to get us some dependable transportation?"

"Talk to Mayor McCullough. He's turned me down four times in the past four months. Open the trunk and I'll help you change it," I told her.

"Well, at least he could give us the money for new tires," she grumbled as she pulled the key from the ignition and unlocked the trunk.

"He won't agree to buy an alternator. We'll never get a set of tires out of him."

Kay made that face that looks like she just walked past a week-old garbage can, and muttered something about Patrick McCullough that I didn't quite catch. Probably should have asked her to repeat it.

"I'll follow you to the PD," I told her, once we had the spare on the car. "I don't know how we're going to explain this to German. If we go ahead and patch the tire tonight, he may never know about it."

"Worth a try," Kay agreed. "He makes such a fuss about this dumb car."

As she pulled onto the highway I noticed that Car 12 was short one taillight and the muffler was hanging dangerously low.

"This is what German found out," Kay said, and handed me the notes in German's handwriting.

Bill had made us a fresh pot of coffee and vacated his chair so that Kay could sit down. I shoved aside the phone log and planted my backside on Bill's desk. "Junk store—where?" I held it out for Kay to read.

"Voster," she said.

"Which would be where?" I asked, holding out the notes again.

Kay read, then interpreted it for me. "South of Nashville."

"German should have been a doctor. So this place has the necklace and ring from the Sikes robbery."

"German had Mrs. Sikes identify it. She says absolutely it's hers."

"But that's all? None of the other stolen items turned up here?"

Kay gave me an apologetic head shake. "Store owner said he didn't remember who brought it in, so it must have been someone he doesn't deal with often. He buys junk and antiques outright, then marks them up. He'd be a lot better off taking goods on consignment, wouldn't he?"

"Yeah," I agreed. "And so would we."

But I was encouraged by German's report. Now that we'd found a few of the items taken in the robberies, there was a good chance more would crop up. German had given the store owner in Voster a complete list of stolen items and asked him to call us if he spotted any of them. He'd also noted that the store owner was scared spitless and would most likely comply with the request.

"Are you finished with that?" Kay asked, pointing to the papers in my hand.

"Sure. Here." I handed them back to her, but she just put them aside.

"You're not going to like this," she warned, picking up another batch of German's notes. "Financial information on the Gentrys."

I read through it twice, looking for any tiny piece

of information I could use to hang Gentry. "Damn,"
I said, when I finished.

"Uh-huh."

"He *is* rich. And so was she." Now, this was the
strangest setup I'd ever seen. Patrice Gentry had a
bundle of money all her own, in her own name, in-
vested in various accounts and mutual funds. Every penny of which went, not to her husband, as
one might reasonably expect, and not even to her
family or friends. She'd left it all to charities. Hell,
the woman had even donated her body to research!

"Come on, Kay," I said, almost ready to beg. "Tell
me he insured her life for a small fortune."

"Oh, she was insured. Bought the policy herself.
A hundred thousand dollars, double indemnity. All
goes to St. Jude's Children's Hospital in Memphis."

"Well, I'm convinced she was an angel. Just like
everybody says. But do you realize the best suspects in this case just became St. Jude's Hospital
and a dozen other charitable organizations?"

Kay gave me a wicked grin. "Let's see you pursue
that. You'll be out of a job in a blink and German
will be the chief of police. And I'll be deputy chief."

For a second I actually considered taking off the
badge. Then I got a grip and remembered that German's first act as chief would undoubtedly be to
ticket me. Bill grinned, probably imagining himself
promoted to patrol officer. That more than anything was enough to keep me in the job.

The Simpleton Party had been out and about. I
could tell by all the campaign posters stuck up
around town. Henry and his friends had plastered

them to every upright surface they could find, and highlighted the posters with crepe-paper streamers. I'd have bet that was Roger Shelton's idea, too.

And sure enough, there was the slogan: FOR SIMPLE VALUES AND SIMPLER TIMES, ELECT A SIMPLE MAN. HENRY MOOTEN FOR MAYOR. I could imagine shivering at the thought a few days before. But driving around on patrol in my own car, wondering how I could wheedle repair money, I felt a strong desire to get to the voting booth. Henry Mooten became my candidate.

Around midnight I was cruising Morning Glory Way, fantasizing about a nap, when I noticed a weak, flickering light shining through Delia's front window. Her car wasn't in the driveway, so I naturally assumed the worst and whipped in there. I eased out of the car, cursing the fact that it was my own and not the patrol car. It hadn't occurred to me to disable the interior light, but I hoped for the best.

I could have used some backup—someone to watch the front of the house while I checked out the back—but that, of course, was an impossible dream.

Delia's backyard is a mess. I mean to tell you. She's got a half-dozen little gardens plunked down wherever they happened to fall, and every one of them marked off by rocks and logs. I nearly tripped over two of the darned things before I got to the back door.

The screen door was standing wide-open and the interior door was opened just wide enough that I could see the shadowy outline of Delia's kitchen table. The beam of a flashlight flickered around inside the kitchen, suggesting that the prowler was headed my way.

The plan was to wait until the wily criminal came out the door, then trip him on the steps, and I'd have my man. I waited patiently, listening to him rummage around inside, looking forward to catching him at last.

It seemed like a solid plan. Unfortunately I heard a noise in the bushes behind me and considered for the first time that there might be more than one burglar. Nearly jumped out of my skin when I turned around and saw two evil eyes glaring at me.

That ugly cat of Kay's had stationed itself in a big old bush and was practically breathing into my nostrils. I don't mind telling you, my heart rate went through the roof.

Now, it only took a couple of seconds to mentally wring the cat's neck and get back to what I was there to do. But it was during those seconds that the burglar started for the door and caught me in his flashlight. I know he must have been as surprised to see me as I was to see the cat, but he recovered quicker.

In no time at all he'd turned tail and run toward the front of the house. I jumped over all three steps and right through the open door, thinking I'd catch him when he stopped to unlock the front door. Still confident, you see, that I had nailed the crook. And praying that for once, Delia had *locked* the front door.

I followed the light trail through the kitchen and

into the living room, where I literally slid to a halt
when I saw the flashlight sitting innocently on top
of a stack of magazines piled on Delia's coffee table.
For one unreal moment I wondered if the damned
thing was moving around by itself, but then, of
course, I realized I'd been duped.

It was like a grade-Z movie and I felt like an id-
iot. He'd tricked me by putting the flashlight on
the table, then hunkered down into the corner by
the door to the kitchen. I figured it out quick, but
he still had the advantage and took it. He was back
through the kitchen by the time I got my feet in
motion, and we both went flying out the back door
with our arms spread like vultures taking off.

When he hit the ground, his legs were already
moving. On the other hand, I landed, grunted,
stumbled, and damned near fell. He kept going.

Even though I knew it was hopeless, I felt like I
had to put on a good show. I kept chasing him
through that plowed field behind Delia's, tripping
over clods and wheezing like an old man. I could
see his arms pumping right along with his legs,
and I noticed that he was wearing some kind of
thin gloves, plus a ski mask that wouldn't even let
me see the color of his hair. While I was congratu-
lating myself on being so perceptive, he gained
three yards.

I've tried every way I can think of to make this
sound like I was a hero, but the simple truth is, I
just couldn't keep up. I still hadn't gotten a decent
look at him, but I was completely convinced that
this was a teenager, or at least a very young man—

and I don't think it's vanity. Only a kid could move like that.

In the distance, I heard a motorcycle start up and figured it might belong to our thief. Still, I didn't want to get my heart set on that, since there'd been no mention of a cycle at any of the other crime scenes. On the other hand, I was a trained observer and the night was quiet and still. Deep in my heart, I felt like I'd found a clue. It didn't make me feel that much better, though.

Once I'd admitted defeat, I limped back to the house and just sat down at the kitchen table, wondering how the hell I was gonna explain this to Delia. I wrote her a note, telling her what had happened and to call the PD as soon as she got home. Then I locked up and went to the PD to get coffee and a candy bar out of the vending machine.

Delia was about as upset as I've ever seen her get. She went tearing through the house, looking in drawers and closets and cabinets and swearing like a sailor all the way.

Hard to believe, but Roger behaved like a grownup for a change. He examined the back door and announced that it wouldn't hold against a hard push, decided that Delia would have to stay at his place until the door was replaced and a better lock added, then obligingly made a pot of herb tea to calm her down.

With all the jars and boxes of weeds she keeps in that kitchen, I don't know how she ever tells what she's brewing up, much less how Roger could tell. I suspected he'd just picked one at random.

Once we got Delia to sit down, she was pretty clear on what had been taken. "Two brooches that belonged to my great-grandmother—I had them on top of the dresser, so they were easy to spot. If I'd put them away, he might not have found them. I don't think he spent a lot of time searching, just picked up anything that happened to be in plain sight."

"Anything besides the jewelry?" I asked her.

"My portable phone—"

"Good," Roger said emphatically. "I hate talking to you when you use that thing."

Ignoring him, Delia kept ticking off items, using her fingers to keep track. "A paperback Stephen King, some herbal preparations, and the pillow from the guest room."

Roger and I looked at each other. "Now, that's strange," he said.

"Tell me." I wrote down everything Delia said was missing, wondering briefly how she could tell. Not that I'd go so far as to call her a bad housekeeper, but she's got her own system, if you know what I mean.

"Why would anybody take a pillow?" she asked me.

"Why would anybody take a paperback when you have all those collectible hardcovers in there?" Roger asked.

"Well, he must have had it all in his backpack. Not much room left in there," I pointed out. "And hardcovers are bigger and hard as hell to bend."

That got a chuckle out of Delia, which made me feel better. Not about letting the little thief get away, but about Delia's state of mind. "Go home with Roger," I advised her. "And if you notice anything else missing, let me know. We're trying our very best to catch this guy, but with only four of us and a murder case—"

"I understand," Delia said. "Just do what you can and I'll cross my fingers."

I left there feeling like an incompetent whiner. Seems like all I do lately is complain about not having enough manpower (don't tell Kay I used that word), not having decent transportation, not having a salary worth mentioning.

Could be my crabby mood has something to do with you being gone. Reckon?

CHAPTER

8

To have and to hold

IT TOOK SOME TIME FOR ME TO RELAX AND shower, and tidy up those little niggly chores like laundry and bill paying, before I could hit the bed Tuesday morning. I hadn't been asleep more than an hour when German called. "Jesus Christ, man!" I remember yelling at him. "What is it this time?"

"Medical examiner's report," he said. "You're not gonna like this one bit."

I figured he was probably right. "What's it say?" I asked, already back into the pillows and half-asleep.

"You sure you want to talk about it over the phone?"

"Yes, damn it, I'm sure. Tell me and let me go back to sleep."

German sighed real heavy, like he was about to tell me something worse than that we had a thief on the loose and that Patrice Gentry was dead and we didn't have a hint of a clue who might have been responsible. "The gunshot didn't kill her," he finally said.

I sat up on the edge of the bed, and asked him to repeat that last.

"The M.E. says she was shot *after* she died. Cause of death was a severed carotid."

I truly and sincerely hoped I was dreaming. All I needed was another piece of puzzle that didn't fit anywhere. I sat up on the edge of the bed and rubbed my face while German shouted, "Chief? Chief?" into my ear.

"I heard you," I growled, and hung up on him.

Going back to sleep seemed like the best way to handle the situation, and God knows I tried. I started on my back, then rolled to my right side, then my left. By the time I was on my belly, facedown in the pillow, I had to admit it just wasn't gonna happen. Times like this I wish I could swallow a handful of pills and let the world take care of itself, but the most powerful medication I had in the house was an old bottle of aspirin that probably wouldn't stop a headache, much less put me into a deep, blissful sleep.

Now that I was awake, I wanted food and companionship. I tried calling you, but you weren't in, so I had to settle for a sandwich and the television. Not nearly as satisfying.

So there I sat, watching June and Ward worry about the Beaver. You reckon there was ever really a family like that one? I don't remember *my* mother wearing high heels around the house.

And you notice they never raise their voices? I tried to imagine Steve and Patrice Gentry sitting down to family dinner, but it just didn't work. Then I tried to picture Ward Cleaver with a harem of bimbos. I know June wasn't the most liberated woman, but don't you think she'd have killed him?

* * *

I couldn't have gone back to sleep if you'd hit me on the head with a sledgehammer. You know how sometimes a song starts running around your head and you can't get rid of it. Worse. You can't remember more than one line, so that line repeats itself over and over until you're half-crazy. Well, that's how I felt.

The same question kept circling in my head— why shoot a dead woman?—and every time I'd try to follow a trail to the answer, it would come back again: why shoot a dead woman?

Maybe somebody wanted to make damn good and sure that Patrice Gentry *was* dead. Although you'd think cutting her throat would have been enough for even the biggest pessimist.

And for Pete's sake, why not shoot her to start with, instead of getting close enough to cut her throat? For that matter, why would someone want to cut her throat? That's pretty damned vicious, isn't it? I mean, pointing a gun and pulling the trigger is almost like not committing murder at all. You could convince yourself that you'd hardly been there when it happened. But a cut throat means a real hands-on type of killer. Somebody who doesn't mind getting blood all over himself.

And having watched Patrice's life run out with her blood, why would that someone bother to go after her dead body with a gun? Unless, of course, we had two people at work here. One who actually killed her, one who came along later and took a shot at her without realizing Patrice was already dead.

Or two people working together, but not well.

I worked on it all the way to Eloise's. The sandwich was still with me, but I thought a big slab of pie might soothe my soul, and I knew I could count on *some*body to be hanging around the diner. In spite of the drawbacks, human companionship is what I need sometimes.

It was too late for the lunch crowd and too early for dinner, so the diner was pretty much mine. That disappointed me. I'd have liked to see Delia, or even Roger.

If Henry Mooten wasn't there, I figured he was out putting up more campaign posters, or maybe going door-to-door. I wondered if he'd thought of a gimmick, like Lamar Alexander's plaid shirt. Maybe I'd mention it to Roger and see if he could think of something for Henry's campaign signature—a space helmet, maybe.

Eloise was sitting on her stool behind the bar, smoking a cigarette and watching the cars go by out front. She waved when I came in and got up to pour a cup of coffee. From the back it looks like she's put on a few pounds, most of it dragging along behind her. Still and all, she's a smart-looking woman. If only she didn't have that sharp tongue and bossy attitude.

"Here," she said, and put the cup in front of me. "Anything else?"

"Sleeping pills," I said. "Or chocolate pie. Whichever you've got more of."

"You want some good advice?" she said, and proceeded to give it without waiting for my answer. "Get a regular schedule."

"Well, why didn't I think of that?" I snapped.

"It's not only good for your system, but you'll be less grumpy. I swear, Reb, you're turnin' into a crabby old coot."

I lit a cigarette and blew the smoke in her face, but she didn't take the hint. "I've just been subjected to too many wedding plans lately. Not to mention evil-do-badders, loony politicians, and busybody waitresses."

She ignored most of what I'd said and all of what I'd implied. "I think it's sweet the way German's taking on. He's in love."

"He's obsessed. Haven't seen much of Pam, though. What's she doing? Hiding out at home until German gets all the work done?"

"You don't know a thing about planning weddings, do you?" Eloise said snidely. "Pam's working full-time and trying to line up a caterer. Not to mention fighting with the florist, looking for a wedding dress, making hotel reservations—all that stuff that drives the bride crazy."

"It's about to drive me and Al crazy, too. They're not getting married till August. How come they have to start so early?"

"If you want it done right, Reb," Eloise said, "you have to start planning early. For one thing, they've both had to get vacations at the same time. Then they've got to reserve hotel rooms, and the preacher's got a schedule, too, you know. A wedding isn't something you just up and have. I know. I've been through my share of 'em."

Indeed she has. If I'd been just a little meaner, or if I'd had just a little more sleep, I'd have pointed out that none of her marriages lasted long enough to justify the time she spent planning them.

"You oughta get a life, too," she went on.

"I tried that once. Didn't work out. Now I've dedicated my heart and my mind to enforcing the law."

Shaking her head, Eloise cut a piece of pie, slopped it down on the plate, and handed it to me. "She's been gone a long time, hasn't she?" she said with more sympathy. "Why don't you take some time off and go see her?"

"Time off." I laughed. "Yeah, I'll just pick my days and leave the department to run itself. Kay and German won't mind a bit working my shift for me, on top of theirs. Ain't like *they've* got things to do, is it?"

"Hire somebody. Give him your salary while you're gone."

"Yeah, and the bank will understand, just like German and Kay will. You seen my stack of payment books lately?"

Eloise propped her hands on her hips and clucked like a mother hen. "Don't give me that poormouthing. You don't *have* anything, Reb. How can you be in debt?"

"I've got a house and a car. The television's going out, the roof leaks every time we get a storm, and I'm saving up for a yacht. Maybe Henry will give me a raise when he gets to be mayor. 'Course, with my luck, he'll pay me in Martian money."

"He might at that," Eloise said. "But it just might be worth the trouble of converting it to dollars. I heard him talking to Frank Pate yesterday. Real serious conversation, too. Henry was saying that they've got to come up with a plan to get reliable transportation for the police. Now, what do you think about that?"

I raised my coffee cup in a salute to the Head Simpleton. "He's got my vote."

After stuffing myself full of Eloise's pie, and fending off her good-intentioned advice, I went back home and stripped down to my shorts for a quick nap. Didn't see any point in going to bed, though, since I sleep better on the couch.

I stretched out there with the clicker in my hand and watched bits and pieces of different shows, hoping to find some kind of private-eye movie. I thought that might give me inspiration, but the closest I could come to it was some murder mystery from the Seventies. That was a bad decade for movies. Not only are the scripts full of goofy language (and I know I used to say *groovy*—don't nitpick), but the clothes will just about put your eyes out.

I was half-asleep when it started again.

Why kill her twice?

I got so tired of chasing that question out of my head that I gave up, got dressed one more time, and went down to the PD to read the report myself. Which, as it turned out, was just as well. When I arrived, German was just putting the phone back in the cradle. "Chief!" he said. "I was trying to call you."

"That figures," I growled. "What now?"

"Well, I'm not absolutely sure about this. But look right here." He pointed to a line in the M.E.'s report.

It said that the bullet recovered from Patrice's body had come from a nine-millimeter.

"Well, German, I'm glad you were gonna call and wake me to tell me this. But I'd much rather have information about the murder weapon, not the mutilation weapon."

"Yeah, but, Chief," he insisted. "Remember the Sikes break-in? That's the kind of gun that was stolen."

Well, by golly. So it was. Until we found the gun and could run it through ballistics, we wouldn't know for sure that it had been used on Patrice Gentry's body. But it sure was interesting. Another loose end to add to the growing pile.

I decided to assume for the moment that it was, indeed, the same gun. Now, why would our burglar want to shoot Patrice Gentry? He hadn't made any effort to hurt me when I'd caught him in Delia's house. On the other hand, I'm a good-sized man and Patrice was a small woman. In addition, she was sitting in her car, and a gun will make a tough guy of a coward.

Had our thief stolen something from Patrice Gentry? And had she tried to fight back? But, no. Not if she was already dead when she was shot.

Well, then, had the thief cut her throat during the robbery and then—I gave up. It was too slippery to hold on to for more than a half second at a time.

For lack of a better idea, I decided to check the possibility that something had been stolen from Patrice Gentry's car. The only way I could think of to do that was to ask her husband. Oh, sure. I

could have sent German to talk to him, but I looked
forward to seeing Dr. Gentry again. Besides, I was
already awake.

Three. That's how many women I found hovering
around Gentry when I got to his house. Not a one
of 'em Amanda or Teresa.

"Now, let me see," I said, ticking them off on my
fingers. "Sheila, Diane, and Patty. Is that right?" I
pretty well remembered them from my Sunday-
morning interviews.

Sheila was a busty blonde who told me that Gentry was a wild man when she got him alone. Diane
was the redhead who said that Gentry was partial
to her back rubs. And Patty was the thin, nervous-
looking one who'd glared at me until I felt the hair
on my neck stand up.

The three of them nodded and Gentry patted
Sheila's shoulder. "These ladies are the salt of the
earth," he said, beaming with pride at his devoted
slaves.

"I reckon so. Sure is nice of you ladies to pitch in
and help out the doctor here. Tidying up, I guess?"
The house was spotless, and I wondered if I could
convince them to hit my place a lick or two. Just
one of the disadvantages of bachelorhood. One of
the very few.

"And sorting out the dishes," Sheila said. "People
really ought to label their dishes when they bring
food." She had a stack of Tupperware bowls and
deviled-egg dishes on the counter. "I don't know
how I'll ever figure out where they belong."

"Sometimes kindness seems more a hindrance

than a help, doesn't it?" I agreed. "Dr. Gentry, I need some help from you. Could we step into the other room?"

All three women sent me warning glances and seemed ready to throw themselves in front of Gentry if I started to drag him off. I grinned to show them I was harmless.

"Of course, Chief Gassler," Gentry said. "Will you excuse us a moment, ladies?"

He led me down the hallway to a room that you'd have to call his study. Dark paneled walls and a big oak desk that looked about as official as anything I've ever seen. It fairly shouted what an important man he was.

Gentry settled into the chair behind the desk and I decided to stand. I didn't like the way he looked so comfortable back there, leaned back in his swivel chair, arms crossed across his chest like he was ready to listen to my symptoms and pronounce a cure for whatever ailed me.

"How can I help you, Chief?" he asked.

I started to tell him about the indigestion that's been plaguing me lately, but thought better of it. "There's some possibility," I told him, "that Mrs. Gentry was robbed. I'd sure appreciate it if you'd take a look through her car, tell me if anything's missing."

Gentry turned gray. "I don't think . . . it would be so difficult," he whispered. "To see where she . . ." He sort of trailed off.

"I understand how hard it would be for you," I assured him. "But it's important. If she was robbed, that could help us get a handle on what happened."

Gentry nodded, pure misery pouring out of him.
"If it can help you find the person who . . . anything
I can do. When?"

"Well," I suggested, "how about right now? While
you've got plenty of folks here to keep an eye on the
house for you?"

He seemed to be casting around for a reason why
he couldn't make it just then, but I guess he didn't
come up with one. After a quick nod he came out
from behind the desk and headed back to the
kitchen to tell the girls where he'd be. I followed,
half expecting Sheila, Diane, and Patty to form a
human shield around the man, but they just took
turns hugging him like he was going off to war.

I took him in my car down to the garage where
Patrice Gentry's car sat next to Kay's patrol car. I
couldn't help but notice the irony—Kay's disabled
Number 7 sitting next to a perfectly good vehicle
that was in the garage only because no one felt like
driving it just now. I also wondered briefly if
Patrice Gentry's alternator would fit Car 7, but
shoved that thought away. I wasn't sure how long I
could resist the temptation if I dwelled on it.

Gentry was reluctant to get out. He sat there in
the passenger seat for a few minutes, just looking
at his wife's car and breathing hard. "She didn't
want the car," he said, more to himself than me.
"She said her old one was fine, and that she'd have
to sell this one before we left anyway. But I insisted. I told her it wasn't safe for her to drive that
old clunker."

Then he stopped talking and put his hands up to

his face. I couldn't tell if he was crying, but I surely hoped not. The last thing I needed was to have to comfort a weepy man, especially one that might have murdered his own wife.

I gave him a few minutes to pull himself together, then opened my door to get him started. In a little bit, he followed me out and over to Patrice's T-bird. He ran his hand across the hood, like he would have done to one of his women. Given his affinity for the opposite sex, I couldn't help but wonder if some guy like Gentry had been the one who'd first started referring to cars as *she*. Wouldn't have surprised me a bit if he'd leaned down and kissed the bumper.

"If you could, sir," I said, trying to spur him on, "just take a look inside. Check the glove compartment, the trunk. Anyplace she kept *any*thing. Try to figure out if there's something missing."

Gentry made a halfhearted search of the glove compartment, pointing out to me what he saw. "Extra pens," he said, "because she hated getting to work and finding herself without one. The owner's manual and an ice scraper. This little emergency care kit that she always carried with her. That's probably all she'd have kept in here."

The trunk was neat and empty, except for the standard jack and spare that came with the car. Either a thief had cleaned it out good, or Patrice hadn't been robbed.

"If you don't mind," I said, figuring I might as well hit it all at once, "we've got your wife's purse back at the PD. Could you take a look?"

Gentry shrugged, as if he'd already been beaten

black and blue, so what did one more smack matter? I had to admit, he seemed honestly devastated. If I'd had one single suspect, I'd have written him off right then. But I sure wished I could figure out how he could love his wife like he claimed he did and still be cheating on her. Annette Gibson's tales of need and fulfillment didn't convince me. For my money, Gentry was scum of the earth and the best suspect I had in his wife's murder. I just wasn't sure if he'd be a throat cutter.

Not that he wouldn't have access to plenty of sharp instruments, and not that he wasn't used to having blood all over his hands. But was Gentry someone who'd do the dirty work involved? No, I figured him for the type to pull a trigger and run.

If I couldn't pin the murder on him, I hoped like hell I'd be able to prove he'd shot Patrice's body afterward.

He dragged along behind me as we went into the PD, like he was a lost lamb following whatever big sheep wandered by. I pointed out a chair and he dropped into it, waiting listlessly while I got Patrice's purse out of the storage closet.

Her purse was like her car—small, neat, and uncluttered. I'd already gone through it, noticed that she carried a wallet with just enough money for vending machine snacks or a tank of gas. Some gum and tissue, a couple of pens with green ink, and a pair of sunglasses. Patrice Gentry traveled light.

I guessed that must have been a habit from her missions of mercy. When you're skipping from airport to ferry to thatched-hut village, you don't lug along the kitchen sink.

"Everything seems to be here," Gentry said, after staring at the contents of the purse for a few minutes. "I'd like to go home now." He sounded like a little kid about to bust into tears.

"I'll take you right back there," I said, and ushered him out to the car.

The silence bothered me. There's nothing in the world as painful as a heartbreak, is there? And this guy's was so strong, I could feel it clear across the car. So I started asking questions.

"I hear you're going off to Somalia," I said.

Gentry didn't seem to hear me.

"That's what your nurse says," I added.

"Oh. I hadn't thought . . . I don't see how I can. Without Patrice. She's always been there, right by my side. No, I can't possibly." He sounded as if he'd just heard the idea, considered and rejected it, right there in the space of a few seconds.

"I can see your point," I said. "Well, Jesus Creek will be glad to have you stick around here. We can always use a good doctor."

"No, that won't do," he said. "Not here. I'll have to get away. You understand."

I understood why he didn't want to stay in the town where his wife had died, where everything he saw would remind him and bring the pain back to the surface. What I couldn't understand was why he sounded like he'd just discovered gold.

After dropping Gentry at his house, I went back to the PD, where German was tucked up at the

desk, making phone calls and checking off items on
his wedding list. Al rolled his eyes at me and motioned me outside to the hall.

"German's nuts," he said simply. Not that he had
to explain it to me.

"What's he up to this morning?"

"Right this minute he's calling a tack shop in
Nashville. You don't think they're gonna have
horses at the wedding, do you?"

An image of Pam doing her Lady Godiva imper-
sonation, riding up to the altar on a big white horse
popped into my head. Ugh. I was sure she had
more dignity than that. I prayed she did, anyway.

Maybe they were planning to arrive at the wedding in a horse-drawn carriage or something. I
surely hoped not. Horses are not my favorite animal, and besides, they get jittery around crowds,
don't they? All I needed was for this ceremony to
break down due to rioting stallions and have to be
rescheduled. Then German would be even more
useless for a longer period of time.

"Keep an eye on him, Al," I said. "Let me know if
you think it's getting out of hand."

"I haven't had access to my desk all morning," he
complained. "You want my opinion, it *is* out of
hand."

I nodded in sympathy. "Listen, Al. I need to get
hold of Jack Sikes. Ask him about that gun of his
that was stolen. If you can move German out of the
way, give him a call for me. Have him get in touch
as soon as he can."

"Will do," Al said. Bolstered by my order, he

marched back into the office and removed German from the dispatcher's chair.

German was still pouting by the time I got my coffee and settled on the edge of the desk to listen to Al's side of the conversation with Jack Sikes. "Very good," he said, in his official voice. "I'll send someone right out."

Al hung up the phone and looked at me. "Sikes says you can get a bullet for comparison out of his bedroom wall. Where the gun went off when he was playing with it."

I shook my head, wondering who was more dangerous—Jack Sikes or the thief who'd taken his gun.

"Okay, German. Go over there and dig out that bullet. And don't stop to make any phone calls on the way."

With German out of my hair, I picked up the M.E.'s report, hoping to find something in that to solve one or more of the puzzles. For the life of me, I couldn't figure out what to make of Dr. Gentry. Call me old-fashioned. If he loved his wife, how come he could fool around with half the women in town?

Sort of like standing in front of the open refrigerator, like you think some new kind of food might pop up there and be just what you're craving. I did that with the report, reading it over and over again until the words didn't even make sense. Nothing.

Patrice Gentry, deceased, had been shot through the windshield of her car. With a gun that *might* have been stolen the night before her death. Prior to that, her throat had been cut with a sharp in-

strument and with some amount of precision. What
the devil did that mean? I wondered. Like, by a
person with medical training? Maybe I could hang
this on Gentry after all.

But if I did, and he got into court looking like he
had every time I'd seen him, what jury would convict? Hell, any female jurors would throw themselves into his arms and offer to comfort him in his
hour of need.

Who else? Amanda Brewer might count. Or any
of the other nurses I'd run into lately. I needed to
know what *precision* meant to a medical examiner.

There'd been dried blood under Patrice's finger-
nails. Probably meant she'd grabbed at her throat
after it had been cut. On the other hand, it could
mean the blood had run all over the place, including there.

I'd have gone on like that all day, probably, if Al
hadn't taken a call right then. Teresa Simmons's
husband had finished his haul and come home to
the news that his wife had been sleeping with another man. He hadn't taken it well. Teresa had
been admitted to the Medical Center and was
ready to press charges.

CHAPTER

9

For better, for worse

I SENT GERMAN TO PICK UP RAY SIMMONS while I went by the Med Center to take a statement from Teresa. Assuming she was in any shape to give one.

She was propped up in bed, looking for all the world like the loser after five rounds with Muhammad Ali. Both her eyes were practically swollen shut, her lip was split open, there was a cast on her wrist, and she winced every time she breathed. Also, Gentry was sitting on the edge of her bed, stroking her hair and whispering comforting words. You couldn't fault his bedside manner. At least, that's what all his women had told me.

"Miz Simmons," I said quietly, and Gentry jumped about a foot. He was off the bed and across the room before I could blink. You'd have thought *he* was the one who'd just been beaten to a pulp.

"Chief," he said, noticeably relieved. "Have you arrested him? Is he in custody yet?"

"Who? Mr. Simmons? We're looking into it. First I need to talk to Mrs. Simmons about what happened."

"Well, for God's sake, hurry," he said. "That man

is a danger to all of us. Just look what he's done to Teresa!" He took her hand gently in his own and touched it with his lips.

Teresa remained silent, but I thought she might have nodded just a bit. She'd know exactly how dangerous her husband was. My only question at that point was how she'd survived the beating.

"We'll do what we can," I promised them both, and the looks of the woman added conviction to my voice. I mean to tell you, she was a sad sight. You've probably seen Ray Simmons around town. He'd make two of me. And Teresa doesn't weigh a hundred pounds soaking wet. What's wrong with a man who does something like that?

"Miz Simmons," I said, easing over toward the bed. "I'll have to hear your story. Can you tell me exactly what happened? Give me as many details as you can remember."

Well, she did, but it wasn't easy for her. Every time she moved her mouth, or even breathed, she'd flinch a little. But she finally got out enough of the story for me to fill out a report and piece together what had happened.

It seems she'd decided not to take my advice and told her husband. As soon as he'd gotten home from the road, he'd stopped off at the Drink Tank to hoist a few with his rowdy friends. Naturally, he'd heard about his wife's affair with Gentry. You know how secrets spread in Jesus Creek. And some good old boy down at the Drink Tank just couldn't wait to stir up trouble.

Simmons didn't take it well. According to her, he came through the door swinging and threatening to kill her *and* Gentry. No wonder the doctor was so edgy.

Simmons had kept on swinging and swigging until he'd passed out on the floor, at which time Teresa had made her escape to the neighbors' and called for help. I figured she was lucky Simmons had been drinking. Otherwise he might not have stopped hitting her until she was dead.

I sure was relieved to know that she was pressing charges for assault.

When I'd finished talking to her and was ready to leave, Gentry stepped into my path. "You should put a guard on the door," he told me. "Until Simmons is in custody. Teresa isn't safe from that monster."

I almost laughed. "Doc," I said, "I can't remember the last time I had any sleep. I've got one officer per shift and we've got more than one active case to pursue. If I could spare somebody, I'd put him on the street. You'll just have to tell the staff here to keep their eyes open. Call us if Simmons shows up here before we find him." Then, just for meanness, I added, "In fact, it might not be a bad idea for you to stay here yourself."

"But, Chief—"

"Honest. I can't do a thing. I've already sent my officer out to arrest Simmons. But I'll tell you the truth, Doc. It won't take him long to make bail and he's likely to be riled when he does."

I'd been whispering and easing toward the door, pulling Gentry along with me. Once we were outside in the hall, I plunged into the other questions that had just occurred to me. "Now tell me, Doc.

Just *where* were you the night your wife was murdered?"

Gentry shuffled around awhile and finally mumbled, "I was with Teresa. I know I said I'd been at home. I'm sorry I couldn't tell you that in the beginning, but you understand now—" He spread his arms, as if there'd been no other course open to him but to lie.

"No. I don't. You lied about your whereabouts. Maybe you don't realize that you're a suspect in this case," I pointed out. "Lying to the police is not a good way to clear yourself."

"But I had nothing to do with my wife's death," he protested. "If you'll recall, I tried to avoid any mention of Teresa. I told you I'd been home alone that night. Now, perhaps that isn't exactly the truth, but you can see why I had to protect Teresa."

"Yeah, but you weren't home all night, and you weren't alone. Miz Simmons says you were with her all night. Is that true? Or is this another story you're using to protect someone else?" Like yourself, I thought.

"Yes. It is."

A rubber-footed nurse hustled down the hall in response to a blinking light and gave the doctor a smile on her way. We both waited for her to get past before we continued.

"You didn't come home around midnight?"

He sighed in resignation. "All right, Chief. I left Teresa's around eleven-thirty and got home shortly afterward."

"Why on earth didn't you tell me this the first time we talked?" And why hadn't he told me just then, when he'd appeared to be 'fessing up to his sins? I wondered if I'd ever get a straight story out of the man.

"Surely, Chief, you can see that I couldn't tell you about this. Why, the man is insane. What was I supposed to do—announce to the world that I'd been with Teresa, even knowing how her husband would react? I'd hoped to avoid trouble by keeping quiet about my relationship with her."

"Avoid trouble? For you or for her?" I jerked my thumb back toward Teresa's room.

"For both of us, of course. That poor, lovely woman is in the shape she's in because—"

"Because you were fooling around with her. Didn't it ever occur to you that her husband would find out?"

"We were very discreet," he said.

"Like you and Amanda? Like you and Sheila? Like you and all the others? Help me out here, Doc. You claim you loved your wife. Kindly explain to me how you could be cheating on her with every female in town." I waited while he drew himself up and tried to cover his tracks.

"You make it sound positively sordid. It isn't. I have deep and sincere feelings for these women. And they for me." He said this, mind, with the kind of sincerity that sells greeting cards. If the man wasn't telling the truth, then he sure was a fine actor.

"Got any deep and sincere feelings for your marriage vows?" I wanted to punch his sanctimonious face, but I just knew every female in that hospital would rush to his defense.

"That has nothing to do with it," he said shortly.

"Oh, yeah? I expect your wife would have disagreed. Unless you two had an arrangement? You think one of her boyfriends might have killed her?"

"How dare you imply such a thing about Patrice! You obviously didn't know my wife or you'd—"

"Excuse me. But if there's nothing wrong with your after-school activities, why couldn't your wife have a *discreet* affair?"

The nurse came by again, but this time the look she gave Gentry was one of concern. She could tell he was being hassled by the mean old lawman and she didn't like it. I flashed her a friendly grin and got ignored for my efforts.

"I can see that no amount of explanation will make this clear to you. And I don't understand why you're standing here harassing me and maligning my wife when you should be searching for a dangerous criminal."

"Good point. I'll see what I can do about Simmons. Just one more thing, though. How well do you know your neighbors?"

"Neighbors?" He looked confused, like maybe he didn't know he *had* neighbors.

"The Barrows. Next door to your house?" I reminded him.

"Oh, of course. Not very well," he said. "Why? What do the Barrows have to do with Simmons?"

"Not a thing," I said, and left.

Everybody had insisted that Patrice Gentry was an angel. It hadn't occurred to me until the words were out of my mouth that she might have been the same brand of angel as her husband. And if she had something going with James Barrow, that would explain why she'd rushed to bail him out of jail.

And if Barrow was scared to death of his wife finding out he'd been stopped for DUI, wouldn't he have been more scared of her finding out about his affair? But, I wondered, would he have committed murder to keep her from learning about that affair?

I thought a man like Barrow might do most anything. And heaven knows people will kill for the silliest reasons. I wanted to pin the murder on Gentry, because he deserved to be locked up for *something*. But the next best choice was James Barrow.

Kay was waiting for me at the PD, dressed in her civvies. "Hey, Reb. Getting any sleep lately?" she asked, and held out a cup of coffee.

"Thanks." I gulped down about half of it. "What are you doing here so early?"

"I had a thought. You know how it is when a brilliant idea pops into your head and you just have to share it? I may know how we can get a lead on the kid responsible for the break-ins."

"Shoot," I said, settling into Al's chair and propping my feet on the desk. I'd have given anything to close my eyes right then and sleep for a decade.

"Dave and Martha Johnson."

I waited a minute for her to explain her reasoning. When she didn't, I asked outright. "They aren't exactly teenagers."

"That's the part I wanted to run past you. You know they've opened their house to the county kids.

About once a month they hold a dance, or a picnic. Last Halloween they put together a hayride and costume party."

"And now you think they've branched out and started a felons' club? Doesn't sound likely to me."

"I know that. This is just a hunch, and don't laugh. Sometimes intuition is real useful. I know one of the kids they've been trying to straighten out. To be honest, Reb, I don't think they can do anything about this one. But even so, it could be that they'd know something. If a teenager is responsible, he must have bragged to his friends and maybe one of them talked to the Johnsons."

"Given that we don't have a thing to go on so far, I'd say you ought to talk to the Johnsons. Just keep it low-key, will you? Don't accuse anybody of anything."

"I'll do it today. Won't even charge overtime."

"Just as well. You wouldn't get—"

The commotion that interrupted my gloomy prediction suggested an impending earthquake, or possibly just a freight train crashing through the wall. Kay and I both jumped to our feet and I'd reached for my gun before we heard German shouting, "Open the door!"

I did, and saw him struggling to hold on to Ray Simmons. Even with his hands cuffed behind his back, Simmons was almost more than German could handle.

I was way too tired to worry about procedure. I just held my gun up where Simmons could see it, pointed it at his head, and said, "Settle down or die."

Really wouldn't have minded if I'd had to shoot.

Al whipped out the key to the cell and German and I together shoved Simmons into it, none too gently. He was lucky enough to stumble onto the cot, facedown. The minute we closed the door he heaved himself up and made a rush for us, looking as if he might go right through the bars.

"Get these things off me," he roared, holding his hands out to the side.

"Not a chance," I told him.

"You can't keep me like this!"

Nothing like having a bear in a cell to make me brave. I gave him my steely-eyed look and said, "Yes, I can." Then I turned my back on him and checked German for injuries. "Looks like a bruise coming up there," I said, pointing to his right cheek.

Rubbing his face and gasping for breath, German nodded. "Won't be the only one. I don't know how I managed to get him cuffed, much less into the car."

"Brutality!" Simmons said, and collapsed onto the cot, moaning.

"Just ignore him," I said. "Sit down, catch your breath, and fill out a report. Don't leave out a single detail, especially if we can use it to prove assault on an officer."

"Fifteen people were watching!" German said. "We've got witnesses to assault."

Kay was hovering over German, trying to determine whether he had other injuries that needed immediate attention. Having decided that he'd live awhile longer, she shot a wary glance at Simmons, still wailing about police brutality. "Is he supposed to be our mascot or something?" she asked.

"Beat up his wife," I told her. "That explains why he's the expert on brutality, I guess. Right, Mr. Simmons?"

Simmons sat up and spat at me. "That bitch needed a lesson," he growled.

"Save it, Simmons. Who's your lawyer?" I hated to mention that, but I didn't want *this* case thrown out of court. "I'll call him and tell him you want him over here."

Grudgingly, he gave me the name of the only lawyer in Jesus Creek and I placed the call. It didn't take Lawyer Maddox long to get all the information he needed and tell me that he'd be right over. He paused just long enough to remind me that I shouldn't question his client until he arrived.

The next item on my want list, after good cars, is a cell separate from the office. We had to sit there and listen to Simmons mutter about brutality and his trashy wife and what he was going to do to *all* of us when he got out.

Trying to ignore him, I updated Kay and German on the Simmons–Gentry love affair and the reason for Mr. Simmons's wrath.

"His wife was having an affair and he finds that *surprising*?" Kay said, amused. "Golly, who wouldn't be satisfied with a man like Mr. Simmons here?" She had raised her voice just enough for Simmons to hear, and he responded with threats against Kay.

"Be careful what you say to my officer," I warned him. "Al, why don't you pull out a tape recorder and get all this down. Just in case any of us trip over a garden hoe in the next few weeks. Our injuries from even a minor accident might land Mr. Simmons in bigger trouble than he's already got."

Al obediently whipped out the recorder and pushed a button. Not that Simmons would have known, but it was a pointless act. That recorder hasn't worked in years.

But after that, Simmons made sure to keep his voice to a level the recorder couldn't have picked up anyway. He seemed to spread his anger around, cursing at his wife, Gentry, and even Patrice for not having been woman enough to keep her man at home.

I wondered briefly if I should add Simmons to the suspect list, but quickly decided that he'd have left a trail of destruction that would have led us straight to him. He was probably the only person in Jesus Creek who was not a suspect in the murder of Patrice Gentry.

Once the lawyer turned up to talk to Simmons, and German had calmed down enough to handle the office, I made a move to escape.

"Are you going home now?" Kay asked.

"Straight there. I've got some mulling to do." And I surely did.

It had occurred to me that if Gentry left Teresa Simmons's house by eleven-thirty, Teresa could have slipped down to the nursing home and done away with the only obstacle standing between her and a respectable man. Such as he was.

The alarm clock must have been ringing for five minutes before I heard it. I managed to get dressed and on the road, but my head was still fuzzy when I went into Eloise's for breakfast, or whatever you call a meal eaten at eleven P.M.

Kay was passing by the diner and pulled in right behind me. She was in uniform this time, officially on duty and fully prepared to protect and serve. "Is there a full moon?" she asked, looking up at the sky.

"Why? Did Simmons turn into a werewolf?"

"You mean that sweet, sweet man down at the PD? The one who cried all afternoon because his wife is in the hospital and we won't let him out to go see her? The man who's so sorry he got upset and can't understand why he's in jail when all he did was lose his temper? *That* Simmons?"

"I wouldn't be at all surprised if that's the one I mean." I held the door open for her and even pulled out her chair before I remembered that I wasn't supposed to do that anymore. I can't help it. It's the way I was raised.

Luckily Kay was too excited to reprimand me for good manners. "Forget Simmons. Wait until you hear this. Anne Barrow is under house arrest!"

"Why?" I asked.

"Well, we've only got one cell and it's occupied. You didn't want me to put her in with Simmons, did you?"

"I meant," I said, trying to keep my voice calm, "why is Anne Barrow under arrest?"

"Assault," Kay said simply.

I closed my eyes and tried to imagine a Jesus Creek where assault was not the order of the day. "Who'd she clobber?"

"Some woman from DHS. The neighbors called it in—not Gentry. The neighbors on the other side. One of the Barrow kids went over to the neighbors to borrow bandages. The little one had cut himself trying to slice a tomato. The kid's only five years old, you know. The neighbor started asking questions and found out that Mom and Dad Barrow hadn't been heard from all day."

"Dandy," I muttered. Goodbye, Ward and June.

"Exactly. Neighbor took a look at the situation, found out the kids were more worried about the blood staining the kitchen counter than they were about the actual injury. The older child said her mom would kill them. Now, we assume this is just a figure of speech, but the neighbor—who has three kids of her own—took the little Barrows home with her and called DHS."

"Since when does DHS act in a timely fashion?" I asked sarcastically.

"Since the neighbor, Mrs. Weldon, threatened them with all sorts of legal action if they didn't. The DHS worker came out to the Weldons. Meanwhile Anne Barrow arrived home, saw the blood, noticed her children were missing, and started going door-to-door. When she got to the Weldons, the DHS worker asked where the devil she'd been while her children were bleeding. This conversation escalated to a shouting match, during which Anne was told that her children might possibly be taken away from her. Then Anne started swinging."

I couldn't help laughing, although I wasn't sure which part of the story was funny. Anne Barrow in her heels and expensive suit, with her polished

house and icy exterior, letting loose with a right
hook should have been scary. Maybe I liked the image because it made her seem a little more human.

"Are there any answers, or just questions?" I
asked.

The night waitress had come over to the table
with coffee and menus and stood there for a while
enjoying our conversation. Figuring the only way to
get our privacy back was to order, Kay did that and
I followed suit.

"Some answers," Kay said. "Aren't you glad?
Okay, Anne Barrow has been off to the riverboat for
the last few days."

"Riverboat?" I asked.

"Gambling casino in Missouri. She told her husband and her employer that she was taking care of
her sick mother, but she had to tell *me* the truth."
Kay was proud of the power her badge carried.

"Don't tell me . . . she was afraid to tell her husband."

"You got it. Once the adrenaline dropped back to
normal, Anne cried and carried on about how her
husband wouldn't understand. She spent a lot of
time blaming him for leaving the children alone,
too. Mrs. Weldon did not hesitate to point out that
had Anne been home where she belonged, the children would not have been alone."

"Good for Mrs. Weldon. What's her first name, by
the way?" I asked.

"Jane. Why?"

"Close. I was hoping for June or Donna. Go
ahead with the story." I sipped at my coffee and
hoped the cook would hurry up with my order.

"By now the woman from DHS had stopped bleeding, but she wasn't in a very good mood. I sent her to the hospital because I thought her nose might be broken. Meanwhile Mrs. Weldon is keeping the Barrow kids at her house because DHS wants to sort out the situation before returning them home. Mrs. Barrow threatened to take them anyway, and that's when I stepped in and ordered her to go home and consider herself a prisoner. Mrs. Weldon knows to call right away if there's any trouble."

Why do you suppose people have children if they aren't going to take care of them? It's easier to prevent it, isn't it? Just imagine what these little kids are gonna be like when they grow up. They'll think it's perfectly normal for parents to hide their dirty little secrets, and to chase after their own pleasure while ignoring the family. Just precious, isn't it?

"I wonder if Mrs. Weldon knows she's walked right into a hornet's nest?" I mused.

"Well, she doesn't seem to care. Jane Weldon is hot about children's rights. So was Patrice Gentry, I gather, but she handled it differently."

"Oh?" I asked, not really wanting to hear any more about Patrice Gentry in this decade.

"This isn't the first time the Barrows have left their children home alone," Kay said ominously. "About a month ago Patrice found them wandering around outside after dark—back when the temperature was still in the teens. The kids had gone out to play and accidentally locked themselves out. They'd slept cuddled up together under the doormat, Reb! Patrice found them out there and took them to her house."

"So DHS already knew there was a problem with this family," I said.

"Nope. Patrice didn't report it. According to Anne Barrow, Patrice understood that these things can happen. She did, however, offer to report to DHS if it happened again. That's why Anne was so furious about her husband being gone. Ever since Patrice's lecture on parental responsibility, Anne has been scared silly that Patrice would turn her in."

"So now that Patrice is dead, Anne Barrow figured she could go off and not worry."

"No, she said she learned a lot from Patrice and realized the error of her ways. She'd insisted that her husband arrange his schedule so that he'd be there when the kids weren't at school. She was ready to kill the man for taking off and leaving the kids this time. And Reb, I really think she meant it. She was just as upset as anybody about the kids being left alone."

"If she was that concerned about her kids being taken away, don't you imagine she might have done in Patrice to prevent it?"

Kay shook her head. "Anne Barrow thinks Patrice was an angel."

CHAPTER
10

From this day forward

I WONDER WHAT THEY DO WITH NEGLECTED
kids in Somalia. Pity we couldn't have sent Mrs.
Weldon over there to straighten out some people.
For my money, she ought to be given an award for
sticking her nose in this time. Maybe it wasn't her
place, and maybe she should have let DHS handle
it, but thank goodness there are still people like
Jane Weldon who are willing to pry into their
neighbors' business.

But the world being what it is, I expect those
kids will be back home within twenty-four hours.

What had become of James Barrow? Kay hadn't
known. She'd asked his wife for her best guess,
but had gotten only a sneer and a cryptic "Who
knows?"

Maybe Carroll County came and got him. Or
maybe he'd been picked up somewhere else and
this time he couldn't find a friendly neighbor to bail
him out. Either way, I didn't mind. He was bound
to turn up soon.

Anne Barrow had told Kay she was grateful to
Patrice for straightening her out, but I doubted it
seriously. It's been my experience that folks don't

take well to having their flaws pointed out. I suspected Anne Barrow would be less open to improvement than some.

Could Anne have been the one who killed Patrice? Trying to prevent Patrice reporting her to DHS? It seemed about as reasonable a theory as anything else I'd come up with so far. Maybe she really did love her kids and, like a normal mother, would have done anything to keep them safe with her. Safe being a relative term, of course.

James Barrow had his reasons, too, for doing in his Good Samaritan. I gathered that he hadn't known about his wife's near escape from a charge of child neglect. Without that for leverage, he might have thought Anne had the upper hand—what with his DUI charges and so forth. Not to mention a possible encounter with an angel. The minute that man pulled into his driveway, I intended to be on his case.

Once I got home and stretched out on the couch, with the television on and the clicker in my hand, a whole bunch of possibilities jumped at me. I turned down the television sound and let real-life drama play itself out in my head.

Teresa Simmons might have been looking for a deeper commitment out of Gentry, but I thought it more likely that she'd been looking for escape from her brute of a husband. A gentle, loving, not to mention well-paid man like Gentry must have seemed real inviting to her. And all she had to do was eliminate the problem of his wife. Well, and her husband, but divorce is fairly common these days. It would have been easy enough for her to dump Ray, but talking Patrice into leaving quietly might have been another matter.

Amanda Brewer was just young enough and idealistic enough to believe that Gentry would marry her if he didn't have a wife to contend with. Gentry himself had already told me he wouldn't be going off to Somalia without his wife. If Amanda could have counted on that happening, she might have killed Patrice to eliminate two problems: the wife and the doctor's departure.

I wouldn't have minded hanging the murder on Ray Simmons, but I couldn't think of a halfway rational motive for him. If he'd been in a killing mood, surely he'd have gone after Gentry, not Patrice. Without a flash of insight to lead me to the killer, I went back to the television, flipping through the channels until I found a John Wayne movie. Now, there was a man who could keep the world and all its children straight. Talk about your solid morality. The good old days, when men were men and so forth. I think it all started going downhill when they shot that first movie in color. Something about the black-and-white image of good guys kept us honest. Now everything we see on the screen just blends in with real life. These days being a hero doesn't require square jaws and good behavior—just Technicolor and special effects.

I started my shift by checking on Mrs. Weldon and the Barrow kids. She's a real comfortable-looking woman—a little round, with fluffy curls that don't look like she bothers with 'em much. She was wearing a sweatsuit when I got there, and a

pair of thick socks. The house was clean, but she'd
left plenty of evidence to show that that house belonged to her family as much as to her—stuffed
animals on the couch, kindergarten art on the refrigerator, and a rented videotape *(The Jungle
Book)* on top of the television.

"My husband's in the garage," she said, drying
her hands on a dishtowel. "Would you like me to
call him?"

"No, ma'am," I said. "This won't take a minute.
My officer told me about the commotion you had
here today. I just wanted to say, I appreciate what
you did. Some folks would have decided it wasn't
none of their business and walked away."

"Children are everybody's business," she told me
firmly. "Those two are sweet as can be, and for the
life of me, I can't imagine how they turned out that
way."

She'd invited me into the kitchen for coffee and
brownies, and naturally I'd accepted the offer.
"They're a little lopsided," she said, without apol-
ogy. "I put the kids to making them after we got
those people out of the house."

By *those people* I supposed she meant Anne Barrow and the officers of the court. I took two brownies and told her honestly that they were delicious.
"I can't believe the kids made these all by themselves."

"They did, though," she promised. "The Barrow
children are used to fending for themselves, I
gather." A little sneer on the end of that. "And mine
help out in the kitchen and everywhere else they
can. Families run on teamwork. Especially when

money's short—like it is around here—we've all got to pitch in to keep things running."

As if to prove it, Mr. Weldon came in through the back door just then, wiping his hands on an oily rag, and gave his wife's head a quick kiss. "Got it to start," he said to her. "Now let's see if it cuts grass. Hey, Chief. Checking up on us?"

"Making sure you don't have any trouble out of your neighbor," I said, and took another brownie off the plate. Weldon looked like the kind of man who could handle most any crisis without raising his voice. I doubted my help would be needed.

"Don't be surprised if we have to call you back," Mrs. Weldon said. "I fully expect that Barrow woman to come barging in here any minute."

"Why?" I asked. "You'd think she'd be glad of the free babysitting."

Jane Weldon stood up and started wiping at imaginary specks on the countertop. Probably nerves. "Oh, any other time I'm sure she would be. But now her possessions have been taken away. It doesn't matter to her that she dropped those kids like week-old garbage."

"I tend to agree with you about Mrs. Barrow. Makes you wonder, doesn't it? People like that with kids they won't take care of. And then on the other side you've got the Gentrys. Fine people from all I've heard, but they didn't have any little ones."

The Weldons shook their heads in unison. "You're right," Mrs. Weldon said. "The Gentrys would have been wonderful parents. We need more like them in this world."

I wasn't so sure about that. One more Gentry

would tie up every woman on the planet and the rest of us poor fools would be doing our own laundry and eating frozen dinners. How many angels can dance on the head of a pin, and how many angels can fit in the town of Jesus Creek?

"Haven't seen anything of James Barrow this evening, have you?" I asked.

Mrs. Weldon threw her hands up in frustration. "Not a hair! According to her"—she nodded in the direction of the Barrows' house—"he could be anywhere. And maybe she's right. I mean, if he was supposed to be home taking care of the kids, and he ran off and left them there—"

"Now, honey," her husband said. "We don't know what's happened to him. Don't jump to conclusions. Could be there was some sort of emergency."

"Well, you tell me"—Mrs. Weldon turned to face her husband—"what possible reason he could have for leaving those children. Name one emergency that would excuse that."

Obviously Mr. Weldon couldn't come up with an answer for that. He reached across the table and took his wife's hand, like an admission that she was right, and also to calm her down.

"Has this ever happened before that you know of?" I asked. I wondered if Patrice Gentry might have talked to them about the time she found the kids locked out of the house.

"I assume Kay Martin told you—" Mrs. Weldon began, but I stopped her with a nod of my head.

"Other than that," I prodded.

"Honestly—and I feel terrible about this—I've never paid attention to the Barrows. They keep to themselves, and the few times I've tried to strike up a conversation, neither of them seemed overjoyed about it."

Didn't surprise me a bit. I couldn't imagine what the Barrows and the Weldons would have had in common, but it might have made a difference if the two families had been friends. Maybe the Barrows would have learned something from their neighbors.

"What about the Gentrys?" I asked. "They'd have been friendlier, I expect."

"Oh, yes," Mr. Weldon agreed. "Just last week, in fact. I borrowed some laundry soap from Patrice Gentry. Caught her in the middle of a phone call, so she set me down at the kitchen table with a cup of coffee while she finished up. Real nice lady. Sounded like she was having trouble getting her passport renewed as fast as she wanted, and if it'd been me, I'd probably have lost my temper. But she hung in there until it got straightened out, then offered me cookies and asked about the girls. I must've spent a half hour there, just chatting, before I finally got the soap powder. A nice woman like that—" He shook his head at the senselessness of her death.

I didn't even want to know why *he* was borrowing laundry soap. And I thought it was interesting that his wife didn't show a trace of jealousy when she listened to the story. I mean, not that Mrs. Weldon isn't an attractive woman, but you'd think she'd be a tiny bit uneasy about her husband being alone in the house with Patrice Gentry.

Or maybe all these crazy relationships have

jaded me. Guess I just don't expect to see trust anymore.

When I checked in at the PD, Bill gave me the report on that bullet they dug out of Jack Sikes's wall. It had come from the same gun that was fired into Patrice Gentry's body.

I thought it was mighty damned lucky for Jack that Patrice was already dead at the time she was shot, otherwise he'd have been an unwitting accomplice to murder. I don't care if the gun *was* stolen. He never should have had it laying out for anybody who came along to pick up. When are people gonna learn to keep their weapons locked up?

Yes, I know kitchen knives make good weapons, too, but that's like saying if automobile accidents happen anyway, why not drive blindfolded? Can we at least *try* to prevent crime?

Expecting a long and boring night, I'd picked up the packet that contained Patrice Gentry's financial records as I left the PD. It was a long shot, I knew, but with nothing better to do, I figured I could take a careful look. The optimist in me was hoping to find some piece of damning evidence that would point to her killer. Just give me a sign, I thought. Point me in the right direction and I'll do my best to get there.

Down at Eloise's, the politicians had gathered. I could see them through the front window when I drove past, with their little heads bent over the table. Frank Pate was scratching away with his pen, no doubt making notes for yet another crazy scheme to get Henry elected.

Maybe I should have suggested they drop the campaign and help German plan his wedding. A UFO theme, maybe. Pam could drop out of the sky, right in front of the altar, with blinking lights on her head. Or maybe that would be better saved for the wedding night.

I took a cruise through town and wound up down by the creek. It was the clearest spring night you ever saw, with a sky full of stars and something like a warm breeze blowing through. I sat out on the hood of the car for a while, remembering when I used to go swimming in that creek on summer nights.

Bet you never did that. My daddy used to round up the neighborhood kids and take us down to the creek. We'd build a campfire and roast wienies on sticks, and marshmallows. Then we'd have to jump in the water to wash off the sticky mess. The water's colder'n hell, and when you first jump in, your whole body freezes up. Then, once you get used to it, it's just refreshing. Puts energy into you and makes you feel tingly all over. Or maybe that's just what happens when you're young. I figured if I'd stripped down to my shorts and jumped in right then, it would've killed me.

Used to dig up crawdads, too. Ugly critters. I never have understood how anybody can eat something that looks like that.

Reminiscing isn't a good idea. I start thinking about how easy life was not so long ago—when everybody knew everybody, when doors weren't locked, and when the church bake sale was reason enough to get dressed up and visit on the side-

walks. I had to shake it off and get back to reality
before I started to cry.

Sometimes, when I'm out patrolling at night and
the houses are dark and the streets are quiet, I get
this creepy feeling that I'm the only one left in
town. I fantasize about how much fun it would be
to have free run of all the houses and stores. Sometimes I try to picture what I might find hidden in
those houses if I could snoop around. You figure everybody's got a secret, right?

King of Jesus Creek. Now, there's a title for you.
Always before, it seemed like a grand thing to be
here by myself, with all the power. But I sat out
there on that creek bank, thinking about being
alone, and it wasn't the same. Another month without you seems like a long, long time. Ever since you
left town, I've had this big chunk of me that's like
the back door's been left open and I'm waiting for it
to be closed.

I piddled around down there at the creek until I
started to feel guilty about shirking my duty, then
made a pass through town. I got to Morning Glory
just in time to see Wayne pulling out of Kay's driveway. Kay was standing at the front door, waving
and blowing kisses. Aimed at him, I expect, and
not me.

I flashed the light once to wish him safe driving,
pulled up to the curb, and walked up to the door.
"Glad he was already going," I said to Kay. "I
wouldn't want to break up anything."

"The poor sweetie's just off midnights," Kay said,
and motioned me on into the house. "That shift

wears him out. No one should have to work like that."

"Tell me," I said, and made myself at home in the living room. Her house isn't quite so neat now that John's not there to tidy up, but I guess if it doesn't bother Wayne, it shouldn't bother me. After all, he's the one who'll wind up stepping over the piles of junk. "Did you talk to the Johnsons yet? Or do you want me to go see 'em in the morning?"

Kay shoved aside her stash of munchies, picked up a notebook from the coffee table and flipped it open, then curled up in a corner of the couch. "I talked to the Johnsons this afternoon," she said smugly. "As well as to some of the kids who were hanging out there. Potato chip?" She held out the bag to me.

"No thanks," I said, noticing that she hadn't offered to share the dip or candy bar.

"Well, the kids don't know diddly, of course. I didn't expect them to open up to me. But Dave and Martha Johnson were wonderful. They listened to everything I said and gave real thoughtful answers."

"But were they useful answers?"

Kay pursed her lips, then said, "Could be. They mentioned two boys who've given them some trouble. Picking up little items around the Johnsons' house. But the Johnsons took care of it themselves, without reporting it to us. They said it's a common problem with troubled teens."

"So are we looking for one of the boys the Johnsons named?"

"They say not. In fact, the Johnsons say none of

the kids they work with would get involved with what they call real crime."

"How involved do they get with our local youth? What, exactly, goes on up there?"

Kay put the notebook down and shook her head. "Best I can tell, they're running a sort of Christian club for troubled teens. Heavy on the self-esteem and guidance, with a smidgen of Bible thrown in. Martha Johnson told me they don't like to push Scripture at the kids, but rather, they try to ease the lessons in a little at a time. She says self-esteem comes first, and then the kids are introduced to the Lord."

"I wonder if the introduction always takes."

"Martha says not. And she's matter-of-fact about it. She told me about fifty percent of the kids don't stay with them more than a week or two. Of the other half, most turn out all right. Of course, not all these kids are problem children. Some are going to be fine anyway, and they come to the Johnsons' parties and prayer meetings because they enjoy it." She picked up that pile of fur she calls a cat and started stroking it. I noticed it had its ears laid back and it was eyeing those potato chips, but Kay didn't seem alarmed. I guess she's lived with worse things than that critter.

"Mighty nice of the Johnsons to devote their lives to helping others," I said cynically.

Kay chuckled. "You sound just like me. I was skeptical at first, but after talking to Dave and Martha, I have to say I'm impressed. They seem to be genuine."

"But not very helpful."

"Maybe more than it seems. I asked them specifically about a kid I know: Scott Carter. He's been in trouble a lot lately, and I'm not surprised. Scott's got an attitude that won't quit, and he's already gotten himself into our files for petty theft, DUI, like that."

"The Johnsons been able to help him?"

"Martha said he comes to the dances occasionally, but never dances. He might turn up for one of the parties, and he's sometimes there for the Youth Prayer Meeting. But he hasn't exactly bonded with the group. Knows the other kids, of course, from school. But Martha said he doesn't have any close friends. She worries about him."

"Sounds like she should. Reckon I ought to go talk to Scott Carter and his parents?"

"One parent. His mother is a nice enough woman, but I doubt she'd be able to control Scott. You're welcome to try to talk to the boy, Reb, but I warn you—he's surly."

"Yeah, well. I'll bet he can't hold a candle to me when it comes to surliness."

Kay raised a warning eyebrow. "Before you get overconfident, I should warn you about something. I asked the Johnsons and they said that Scott is left-handed. If he's the one who's responsible for our break-ins, he's armed with custom-made firepower."

I cruised through town a couple of times, keeping an eye out for criminal activity, but mostly hoping to find James Barrow's car parked in his driveway. It got to be damned frustrating, so I decided I'd

make a point of finding out exactly where he was
and how to get in touch with him, first thing in the
morning.

The boy Kay had mentioned, Scott Carter, would
have to be checked out, too. I'd noticed she hadn't
offered to talk to him herself, but I hadn't pushed
it. Kay's always eager to do her job and everybody
else's. If she didn't want to tackle this boy, I knew
she had a good reason.

She'd given me directions to his mother's house
and I drove past, but all the lights were out and
there was no good reason for me to wake folks. I
crossed my fingers, though, hoping I'd get back
there in the morning and find a motorcycle loaded
down with VCRs, computers, and maybe a couple of
peanut-butter-sticky prints on the handlebars.

Around two o'clock, bored out of my skull, I
pulled up to the courthouse and used my flashlight
to go through Patrice Gentry's will and bank statements.

Sure enough, the will left every penny to good
and charitable causes. What an angel. The statements showed that she was about as financially
solvent as anyone I'd ever heard of. She actually
had a balance on the plus side every single month.

Of course, this was only what we'd learned from
the Jesus Creek bank, and the Gentrys hadn't been
in town all that long. I was hoping for something to
show up when we got the records from their old accounts.

Meanwhile I still had her personal records that
we'd borrowed from the house right after her
death. Somehow going through those seemed inde-

cent. The dead woman's life all tied up with string and like that. I felt like a peeper, but if I hoped to bring her killer to justice, I'd need all the information I could get. Surely Patrice Gentry would forgive me and understand.

Dumping the contents of the envelopes one at a time, I glanced through the canceled checks. Ordinary expenses, like electric bills and so forth. A couple of checks made out to the uniform shops in Nashville. Patrice wasn't a big spender, it seemed. Sensible with money. It occurred to me we ought to check out the doctor's records and see if he was as thrifty as his wife.

I couldn't help smirking when I ran across the check Patrice had written for James Barrow's bail. Imagine being so scared of your wife you'd rather drag a stranger into the matter. The little Devil Reb popped out of my head and said: Show it to Anne Barrow. But of course the Angel Reb stomped on that idea. Too bad I'm a naturally good guy.

CHAPTER

11

For richer, for poorer

AT SIX A.M. I MADE ANOTHER PASS BY THE Carter house out on Dead Branch Road. The lights were on and I could make out the shapes of people moving around in the house. I hated to bother anybody that early in the morning, but I wanted to find out about this boy Scott before any more time passed.

Please, I prayed, let him confess to the burglaries. I was willing to beg harder, but by the time I'd parked in their driveway and gotten out of the car, the front door of the house had popped open. Two little girls of the snotty-nosed-brat variety tumbled out, took one look at me, and scurried back inside. It was only moments before a frowzy blonde came tearing out the door, straining her polyester pants and heading for me just as fast as her feet would carry her.

"Reb!" she said, already out of breath. "What is it? What's wrong?"

It's the first time I'd ever seen Lola that excited. Back in school she was always the kid picked last for any team. We never knew whether she could play or not—she never moved fast enough for us to find out.

Another thing about Lola that came to me just then was that she'd married some soldier and moved away. When she was about fifteen, as I recall. We all knew it wouldn't work, so it was no surprise when she came back to Jesus Creek with a bunch of kids in tow. I *was* surprised by how much she'd aged, but then, I guess I don't look quite like I think I do, either.

"Calm down, Lola," I said, holding her by the shoulders to keep her from plowing right into me. "Nothing's wrong. No more than usual. I just wanted to talk to your boy."

I swear that's all I said to the woman. So I was completely stunned when she burst into tears right there in the yard. I had to pull a handkerchief out of my pocket and it wasn't all that clean, but she didn't seem to notice.

After Lola had wiped her tears and gotten her voice under control, I asked again. "Could I speak to your son, Lola? I just want to ask him a few questions."

"That's just the thing, Reb," she said, still sniffing. "Scott's gone. I haven't seen or heard from him in over a month. He's a stubborn boy. I just don't know what to do with him anymore."

This brought on a fresh river of tears. I waited patiently, patting her on the back, while she got it all out of her system. I hoped. Meanwhile the brats were peering at us from the open front door.

"You mean to tell me Scott's missing?" I asked her. "Why on earth didn't you report it to me?"

"Well, he's almost eighteen, Reb. I guess the boy can go where he likes. And up until last week I thought he'd gone to stay with the Johnsons up at the old Tyler place. He's been spending a lot of time there. But I finally decided his tantrum had gone on long enough, so I just drove up there and was gonna tell him to come home that instant. Only the Johnsons said he hadn't been there in a couple of months. And now I don't know where he is." She started to wail and blubber, all the while carrying on about how hard she'd tried to be a good mother and how worried she was that Scott had met up with trouble.

I stayed only as long as I felt I had to, then promised Lola I'd conduct an all-out search for her son. She'd told me he had a motorcycle, but she didn't know the license number. Assuring her that I could find out, I advised her not to worry, hinted that teenage boys pull this sort of stunt all the time, and lit out of there like a cat with its tail on fire.

I stopped in at the PD in time for change of shift and dropped off the financial records I'd carried around all night. A quick check with DMV told me that Scott Carter's motorcycle didn't have tags—at least not legal ones—making it a tad more difficult to find him than I'd expected. I updated the dispatcher on that problem, asked him to spread the word to the other shifts that we wanted to talk to Scott Carter, and went in search of my deputy.

German was out front, poking around under the hood of Car 12.

"Giving you trouble already?" I asked him. "Hell, you just got to work."

"I think Kay's done something to it," German whined. "It won't idle. Keeps dying on me. I wouldn't put it past her to do the same thing to my car when we leave for our honeymoon."

I walked around the car, kicking tires and praying for a miracle, while German tugged on various wires and cables. Finally he pulled his head out again and slammed down the hood. "Well, *I* can't find anything wrong with it," he said, disgusted.

"Use your own car," I advised. "Why not? The rest of us have to use ours."

"When are we going to get—"

I held up my hand to stop him. "Tell it to the mayor. I've talked till I'm blue in the face. Right now I'm headed for Eloise's for something to eat. Then I'm going home and I don't want to be disturbed. I don't care what happens, I do not want to wake up before I'm ready. Got it?"

German nodded grudgingly, still ticked off about his patrol car not running. He's way too attached to that car, in my opinion. Maybe I ought to warn Pam about this.

I decided to walk over to Eloise's and enjoy the morning. The sun was already out and shining to beat the band. The trees seemed to have gotten greener overnight, and I could smell spring in the air—that sweet, fresh scent that means it's okay for us to store the wool and start making plans for cookouts. Tired as I was, I still had energy left over to appreciate nature's effort.

Henry and Frank weren't at their usual table,

which I took to be a sign that God was handing me special favors. Benny and Chester had just dived into their breakfasts and they both grunted good morning to me. Eloise was bustling around behind the counter, setting up for the rush to come. I took a stool and slid the ashtray closer to me. "Take a break and join me," I said to Eloise.

"You twisted my arm." She pulled her own pack out of her skirt pocket and leaned over the counter so I could light her cigarette. "You look like you've just come off a three-day drunk," she said charitably.

"That would have been a lot more fun. Life's so full of niggly problems, I don't have time to live it." I picked up the menu and glanced over the options, kind of feeling like I was in the mood for something different. Of course, I've been eating there so long now, there's not a single item on the menu I haven't had at least three dozen times, so I gave up right away. "Just whip up whatever you think I want," I told her.

"I know exactly what you want," Eloise said with a grin. "But she's not here. You'll have to take breakfast instead."

She jotted something down on her order pad and passed it to the cook, then nodded toward the front. "Trouble coming," she warned.

I turned in time to see German saunter through the door. He was headed straight for me.

"Whatever it is, I'm out of town," I told him.

Plunking himself down beside me, German shook his head. "Don't worry, Chief. It's nothing big. Steve

Gentry just called the PD, wanting to know if he can leave town."

"Man watches way too much television," I said. "Tell him he can leave, just so long as he's back here when I want him."

"That's the problem, Chief," German said, with a strained look. "He wants to leave for good."

"The hell he does," I said.

"Yeah, well, I figured you'd react that way. I told him you'd be in touch when it was convenient for *you*." German was proud of himself for thinking fast. I could tell by the silly grin on his face.

"Good job, boy," I said, but avoided the temptation to pat him on the head.

"Hey, Chief?" he said. "You're not allergic to flowers, are you? Pam says if you are, we'll get you a silk boutonniere."

"Allergic to everything that grows," I said. "Even silk."

I put German back on the road and prepared to enjoy my meal in the relative peace provided by Eloise's. That place is starting to look more familiar to me than my own house. Surely more comfortable than the PD.

I tried relaxing there once when it seemed like I'd turned into a couch potato at home. I remember it lasted about ten minutes. Then Kay came in and decided I must be depressed or something. She wanted me to talk to her about it. Kay is convinced I'm tormented by horrible memories of Vietnam. She figures I saw so much ugliness there that I've got a real perspective, or some kind of special wisdom or something. Thinks I don't fret the small

stuff. I'd like to straighten her out—let's not per-
petuate the myth, I figure—but then I'd have to
explain the truth.

After that, I didn't want to hang around anywhere I could be cornered alone. At least at Eloise's
there's always somebody to put between me and
Kay's misunderstanding or German's wedding
plans.

Another thing about Eloise I like—she's older
than me. She remembers the good old days. Sometimes you just need to talk to somebody who understands why it was normal for Kennedy to be riding
in an open car.

I took my time with breakfast, then had a couple
more cigarettes with Eloise. After that I had a lei-
surely stroll back to the PD and collected my car.
Truth was, though, I was curious. Patrice Gentry
had been dead a few hours short of a week, and her
husband was ready to leave town. I wondered why.

When I pulled into the Gentry driveway, I noticed right off that Gentry's car was loaded down
with clothes and suitcases. He'd been pretty confident, I guessed, that I'd give him the okay to pull
up stakes. Maybe he was planning to take off no
matter what I said.

I knocked politely on the door and waited for him
to open it, then stalked in like I was conducting a
raid. "Leaving us?" I said. It came out sounding
rough, due to my sleep-deprived, nicotine-trained
throat, but I didn't apologize.

"Chief," he said, with relief. "I've been trying to
get in touch with you all morning."

I looked at my watch. "It's barely eight-thirty. Looks like you've done enough packing while you waited for me. Got everything? Clean underwear, passport, traveler's checks?" The living room was cluttered with clothes and personal items, and a couple more suitcases were open on the floor.

"Passport?" he said. "That's expired. Besides, I don't have time for a vacation. This is far too important for that." Gentry seemed confused, like he thought I ought to know what he was talking about. "I got a call last night from a major hospital in Houston. I've been trying to nail down this position for weeks now, and they've finally given me an answer. It's an enviable position. The sooner I get there and get settled, the sooner I can get to work."

"That important?" I whistled. "You can't take a few more days to clear up the matter of your wife's death?"

He had the grace to look ashamed, but he kept on throwing shirts into a suitcase. My guess was that he'd heard Ray Simmons had made bail. That sure would motivate him to move fast.

"Besides that," I pointed out, "you've got a business here. Can you just walk away from your patients at the hospital? Not to mention your clinic."

"Dr. Finster has agreed to cover for me at the hospital," he said shortly. "I've asked Amanda to close up the clinic. She knows what to do." Then, proud as a banty rooster, he added, "And I've taken care of her, too. I've arranged for her to have Patrice's job at the nursing home."

Thoughtful of him to take care of one of the mistresses. I would have liked to ask what he was doing for all the other women he was leaving behind, but I figured the answer might take all morning.

The sad truth was, I had no legitimate reason to keep him in Jesus Creek. "All right, Dr. Gentry," I said. "Before you leave town, I want you to stop off at the PD and leave us a number, an address, and the name of this hospital. Be sure to give us the administrator's name and number, too. If you fail to do this, I will send a pack of law hounds after your butt. Understand?"

"Yes, yes," he said, barely paying attention to me. "Thank you, Chief. Now, if you'll excuse me, I have a lot to do."

I stood there watching him, wishing he'd make a wrong move. After a couple of minutes, during which he ignored me as completely as if I'd never existed, I made my exit.

All the way home I pondered it. Gentry had said he'd been working on getting this new job for weeks. Why? If he'd been planning a trip to Somalia, he couldn't very well have taken a new job here in the U.S. Ergo, I said to myself, he never intended to go to Somalia. So why didn't he just say that in the first place, instead of making up a bunch of bull about how he couldn't face it without his loving wife by his side?

I almost circled back to ask him, but my eyelids felt like somebody'd sandpapered the inside of 'em. A bed, even an empty one, seemed more important than needling Gentry.

* * *

Maybe because it was the one-week anniversary of Patrice Gentry's death and that was naturally on my mind, I dreamed about the nursing home. It was one of those crazy, scary, frustrating dreams that kept changing. Everything made sense while I was asleep, mind you, but once I woke up, it was a hodgepodge of images. First I'd been out in the parking lot, talking to Patrice through her car window, except she was already dead, and in the dream I never noticed. Thinking about it after I woke up gave me the willies.

Then I floated like a ghost inside the building, where the sound had been turned off. I could see patients moaning, but couldn't hear a peep. Diane Forsythe came barreling down the hall, pushing a heavy cart full of medicine and needles, but it was completely silent. Even when she smiled at me and said hello, I couldn't hear her. And while I was dreaming all this I thought the nursing home must be soundproofed to prevent cars outside waking up the patients at night. I remember wondering if they turned off the soundproofing during the day.

There was a lot more to it—it seemed like I dreamed for twelve hours straight—but this is the part that's important.

I know the scientists who do dream research say we'd all go nuts if we didn't dream, but here's one man who's gonna lose it if he doesn't get some undisturbed sleep soon. Trying to get showered and dressed took every lick of energy I had. I figured part of the problem had to do with being at a loss to find answers to any of our current mysteries. Who killed Patrice Gentry? Who killed her again?

Who was breaking into houses and stealing deadly weapons and peanut butter?

Kay was waiting for me at the PD, hanging over the computer with Bill reluctantly explaining something to her. He doesn't much like the way Kay's showing interest in learning how to operate it.

What worries me is her obsession with the job. I swear, she can't stay away from the place even on her off day. And she was dressed to kill, too.

"Big date?" I asked, trying not to let her know I thought she looked mighty fine.

"Party for Pam," she said. "We had a personal shower for her. I know it's a little early, still, but everybody's leaving on summer vacations soon, so this was the only time we could do it without running into scheduling problems with vacations or the regular wedding showers or the wedding itself."

"Still months away," I pointed out. "What if they call off the wedding?"

"Don't be silly, Reb," Kay said, shaking her head. "They're not going to do that."

I saw a chance to get some advice, so I took it. "What sort of gift do you think they'd like?" I asked. "Reckon I could put money in an envelope and slip it to German at the wedding?"

"You could," Kay said, but I caught the way her lip curled up.

"What did *you* get, then?" I asked sourly. Women are always such know-it-alls about gift giving.

"Remember this was a personal shower for Pam," she said. "I gave her printed stationery, with her name and a tiny rose on it."

"Now *that* could be a waste of money," I pointed out. "Suppose they do call off the wedding. What good's it gonna do her to have a boxful of stationery with *Pam Hunt* printed on it?"

"It doesn't say *Pam Hunt*," Kay explained. "It's *Pamela Satterfield*. Even if German screws up big time, she can still use this gift."

"But she has to use it before the wedding? I don't get it."

Kay laughed in my face. "You nitwit," she said. "She'll still be Pam Satterfield after the wedding."

Now, I've been aware for some time that women are keeping their maiden names after marriage, but I had no idea that crazy fad had invaded Jesus Creek. Leave it to Pam.

I gave up on trying to talk sense to Kay about wedding gifts. "So what brings you here on your day off? And after hours, too?"

"I thought I'd let you know: I dropped by the Weldons' this afternoon to see how the Barrow kids are doing. DHS moved really fast and the kids are back with their mother."

"Sorry to hear it," I said. "But you didn't have to make a special trip to tell me. I can't fight DHS."

"There's more news," she pointed out. "Naturally I went by the Barrows', just to be sure the kids weren't alone again. Anne Barrow positively chuckled with glee. She's found out about her husband's trouble down in Carroll County. I swear, Reb, she's like a kid pulling wings off flies. It tickled her to death that the man's in trouble."

"And what did he have to say in his defense?" I

asked, wishing I'd been there to see it when Anne Barrow confronted her felonious husband.

"He's still gone. Anne was giggling about that, too. She said something to the effect that he'd wimped out. That he was scared to face her knowing that she 'had one on him.'"

"Is this what we're supposed to call a dysfunctional family?" I asked.

"Boy, if it's not, I'd hate to see one. She wasn't the least bit concerned about the trouble she's in with DHS. I got the impression that it's a game—I get some dirt on you, you get some dirt on me, and the one with the biggest pile of dirt wins."

We both just shook our heads, trying to make sense of that couple. "Wonder where Barrow is?" I mused. "Not that I blame him for getting out of there, but maybe his timing could have been better. Disappearing when you're facing charges doesn't look good."

Kay studied on that for a while, then asked me, "You don't suppose he's in bigger trouble here in Jesus Creek? Patrice Gentry's death, for instance?"

"Is he left-handed?" I asked her. "Can we pin the burglaries on him?"

"Worth a shot. Shall I run him through the computer?" Kay made a start for the blasted contraption, but Bill stopped her.

"*I* work the computer," he said testily.

"A little discreet digging might be in order," I agreed. "Don't go all out. We don't actually want the man for anything. Yet. Meanwhile I've got more disturbing news. I dropped in on Scott Carter's mother this morning."

Kay sighed. "That poor woman. What did Scott have to say?"

"Scott's missing, too. Lola says he's been gone about a month, but she'd thought until last week he was staying with the Johnsons. He wasn't. Keep an eye out for the boy. If you spot him, run his tags. That'll give you a reason to haul his butt to the curb. We'll question him about the burglaries then."

"Well, with Scott and Barrow both missing, we might want to consider them suspects in the murder case, too. Just until we're sure."

"You don't reckon a kid like Scott would be involved in murder, do you?"

Kay gave me a look. "Have you ever met Scott?" she asked.

"I'm fairly sure not. Why?"

"Hmmm," was all she said.

"Besides, I've still got my heart set on nabbing Steve Gentry." I updated Kay on that story.

"He's taking a job in Texas?" she asked. "What happened to Somalia?"

"Told me a while back he couldn't go there without his loving wife along," I explained. "But what I don't understand is why he was even considering going to Somalia when he'd applied for this job in Texas. I remember Mr. Weldon mentioning that Patrice was working on getting her passport back before she died, but Gentry told me himself *his* was out of date. Evidently he hadn't done squat about getting it renewed. I'd think that would take a long time to arrange."

"Only three weeks or so. When were they planning to go to Somalia?" Kay asked.

What does she know about passports? I wondered. "Beats me, but passport aside, he's got this new job he's been working on for several weeks. Would you apply for a job just before leaving the country?"

"No," Kay said. "What do you suppose this means?"

"Beats hell out of me. I haven't understood anything since they canceled *The Ed Sullivan Show*."

Not even food could improve my mood, so I skipped Eloise's and drove out to the nursing home. I parked way over by the edge of the lot so I could get a full view of the lot and the cars in it. The space where Patrice's car had been parked when she died was occupied by a junky old pickup. I don't know why that bothered me. I guess I'd been thinking of that spot as a kind of shrine to the angel.

A week's time had passed and all manner of information had been gathered, but I felt like my brain had been scattered to the winds. If I could have concentrated on the murder, maybe I'd have the killer by now. But with all the trivial shit going on around me, I couldn't follow one thought to its end before somebody came at me with another problem.

Sitting there that night, I almost heard Patrice Gentry's voice, blaming me for not paying enough attention to her. I tried to imagine what she'd been like. Nobody's an angel, I reminded myself. *Had* she had a lover? Or was she blindly in love with her husband? The photographs I'd seen of her sure made her look good. The kind of woman you'd expect to be working with sick old people. Real gentle light in her eyes.

I imagined her meeting Gentry, and wondered what it was about him that made her fall for him. Maybe he hadn't been a womanizer back then. After I'd seen him with that little girl in the emergency room the day I went to tell him his wife was dead, I could see that Patrice would have found him a kind and compassionate man.

But you don't live with somebody long before you find out their flaws. And I doubted Patrice was dumb. She must have known about his other women, even if *he* thought he was being discreet.

What do you reckon makes a man cheat on his wife? Especially a looker like Patrice. And it's not like he found one woman to fall in love with. The guy just seemed to be in it for conquest. Some kind of power trip is what I finally decided it had to be. Pretty damned childish, yeah, but who says people have to behave like grownups when they pass the age of twenty-one?

For a good example, look at the Barrows. Hell, look at German and the goofy way he carries on, or Henry Mooten playing make-believe with space aliens.

That thought reminded me of Miss Constance and the alien she'd seen right there in the parking lot. It made the hair stand up on the back of my neck, and I have to admit, I took a quick look around me, just to be sure I was alone. I gotta get some sleep.

It occurred to me that I'd found a good place to nap, but that night I didn't dare fall asleep. Those crazy dreams from earlier might have come back and I was in no shape to put up with that. So I just sat there, hoping to stave off dead women and wacky thieves and anything else that might cause further digestive upset. And wouldn't you know, that's when it came to me.

Remember I said I'd dreamed about the nursing home being soundproofed? Well, it just about is. When I talked to Diane Forsythe that night, she'd said she hadn't heard a thing that went on in the parking lot, not even when her own car had been vandalized. And I'd noticed myself that when I opened the door to leave that night, all the sounds came rushing at me. When I'd been inside, it was like a tomb. If you don't count the sounds of old people moaning.

So how come, I had to ask myself, Diane Forsythe said she'd heard the shot the night Patrice was killed and mistaken it for an accident inside the place? I couldn't remember if she'd said definitely that it had been the shot, or if she'd decided that's what it was after she learned about Patrice's death.

Sure seemed like I'd better nail that down.

CHAPTER
12

Till death do us part

FINALLY I WAS GETTING A BREAK. UNLESS it happened to be her night off, Diane Forsythe should have been on duty right then. All I had to do was walk inside and ask her.

But I couldn't do that, could I, when the doors are kept locked during the night shift. I was pondering that, realizing if I had a real patrol car I could've radioed Bill and had him phone the nursing home and tell Diane to open the door for me. But there I was, stuck in my own personal transport, without a lifeline.

Knocking on the door would probably scare the poor woman out of her wits, and then what would she do? Why, call the police, of course. Meaning me. But I'd never know it because I was stuck in a car without a radio.

I puzzled over that for a few minutes when, once again, God showered me with blessings. The back door of the nursing home opened and out stepped Diane Forsythe. She already had her cigarettes out of her coat pocket. Thank heaven for addictions, I thought, and started to get out of the car and hail her.

But the newly repaired security light bounced off
something at the edge of the parking lot. I swiveled
around in my seat for a better look and nearly
passed out. Coming through the woods to the side
of the nursing home was a silver-helmeted alien.
Short, just like those tabloids always describe
them, and gliding like its feet weren't even touching the ground.

Of course, I got my wits back right away and
realized it was no visitor from Mars, but just somebody coasting in on a motorcycle. I mentally con-
gratulated him on having the sense to wear a
helmet, at the same time wondering why he'd cut
the engine. And why was he coming through the
woods instead of coming up the drive like any sane
person would have done?

Whoever it was rolled right up to Diane Forsythe, who did not seem in the least disturbed. And
then he removed his helmet—with his *left* hand—
and propped it on the handlebars before getting off
the bike.

My, my. God sure *was* being benevolent to me. I
desperately wanted to get close enough to hear the
conversation, but I couldn't open my door without
the interior light alerting Diane and her visitor to
my presence.

I reached up behind me and tried to disable the
light without taking my eyes off the action in front
of me. Diane and the rider seemed to be having a
serious discussion about something, but she wasn't
afraid. If anything, *she* was the one in charge
there.

It's easier when you're looking at what you're

doing, but I managed to pull the interior light cover loose and flip out the bulb. The next obstacle was getting out of the car without making noise. I gently, gently rolled down the window just enough to let the night sounds in. All I needed was a passing truck to drown out the squeaky door, but barring that, I'd take any loud vehicle I could get.

God must have decided I'd exhausted my share of favors, because all I heard from the highway was silence.

Meanwhile Diane and the rider kept stepping around, moving back and forth, and in the process, putting parked cars between them and me. I could see her pulling something out of her pocket and handing it to him, but couldn't make out what it was. Looked like little items tucked into a clear plastic bag.

I didn't think they'd take a walk in the woods together, but I still wasn't convinced that she was safe out there. Tough lady though she was, Diane Forsythe might have been conversing with a killer, for all any of us knew. I went ahead and unbuckled my holster.

I don't like the feel of that gun in my hand. Having it there, at the ready, makes it too easy to pull the trigger when another option might have worked. Still, I felt like I needed to have the upper hand in this case, so I went for the artillery.

Whatever they were talking about, they were keeping it low. I couldn't even hear a murmur on the wind. With the gun in my right hand, I used my left to open the door just a fraction. The click it made when the latch let go sounded deafening to me, but Diane and her buddy didn't even glance in my direction.

I waited as long as I could stand it before pushing the car door open just enough to let me out. Then I tried to keep my knees bent so they wouldn't see my head sticking up above the car line. It's about as uncomfortable as I've been lately. Maybe I ought to get Delia to teach me some of that yoga she's so big on.

Much as I wanted to avoid being seen, I wasn't about to get down on my knees and crawl between the cars. But by the time I'd crouched my way up one row, my legs were screaming like they were on fire. I was in agony and all of a sudden I heard Diane Forsythe laugh. That really ticked me off.

So I stood up. Straight up, all six-feet-odd and started toward them, with my gun hand down at my side. I was being cool, pretending there was nothing unusual about all of us being out in the parking lot in the middle of the night.

Diane saw me first and said something to the rider. Sounded like "go," but I wasn't sure. Whatever it was, it got him moving. He straddled the bike, kicked it, and took off like a bat out of hell. His helmet fell off the back of the seat and bounced on the asphalt twice before it rolled over to Diane's feet. She just stood there, paralyzed, her cigarette halfway to her mouth and her other hand in her pocket, like she was modeling for Philip Morris.

There didn't seem to be any point in chasing a motorcycle on foot, so I let it go. Walked right up to Diane Forsythe and picked up the helmet. It was fairly new, bright and shiny, with a name painted on the front. *Jason.*

"Last name?" I asked Diane, holding out the helmet.

"I wouldn't know," she said coolly.

"Friend of yours?" I asked.

"He's a passing acquaintance. I have to get back to work now." She tossed the half-smoked cigarette on the ground and stepped on it.

"Why did you tell him I was out there?" I asked. "And why did he take off that way?"

"He was leaving anyway," she said with a shrug.

"Didn't seem to be in a great hurry until he saw me," I pointed out. "Expensive helmet he's left behind here, too. Now, you and I both know something was going on here. And you *ought* to know I'm not gonna leave it alone. Why don't you tell me the whole story?"

We tried staring at each other for a while, but that didn't get us anywhere. "What was that you gave him?" I asked her. "You selling off prescription drugs?"

"No," she said firmly.

"What then?" I didn't expect an answer. After all, what else could it have been but drugs?

Surprised me when she piped up right away. "It was minor supplies. Alcohol, iodine, disposable syringes. Not drugs. I would never be a part of that."

Talk about confused. "Why on earth would you be swiping alcohol from the nursing home and passing it on?"

She seemed to loosen up then, realizing, I guess, how silly it was. After all, what's a bottle of alcohol? "That happened to be what I gave him to-night," she said. "There's a list. Bandages, alcohol, aspirin, scalpels—basic medical supplies. Sometimes antibiotics or painkillers."

"Is this guy starting his own clinic or something?" I couldn't for the life of me imagine what either of them had in mind.

"I haven't asked what he does with those things. I don't care."

Standing there under the security light, she couldn't have missed the way my mouth dropped open. Not a single explanation bothered to come to my mind and I was straining for one.

Diane Forsythe grinned at me. "He does what I ask of him. That's all that matters."

"And what do you ask?"

"He pays me," she said. "A nurse's salary isn't enough to cover more than the basics. Once in a while I ask for the item rather than the money it brings. A VCR, for instance. I've always wanted one. I love movies, but I'm stuck on this shift, so I never get to watch them in the theatres. And I couldn't afford to buy a VCR. Not after I pay rent and utilities, the car payment . . ." She sighed. "Life is so expensive."

"So this Jason burglarizes houses, then sells what he steals—or just gives it to you—and in return, you steal medical supplies for him? How much did he get for those towels he stole? Or the plastic plates?"

Diane shifted her weight, suddenly bored with the conversation. "I don't care how he gets the money," she said.

"Tell me this, is a VCR worth jail time?" Not that I thought she'd really go to jail, but at best she'd lose her job and her reputation.

Her hand came out of the coat pocket with a gun in it. A nine-millimeter that most likely had been stolen from Jack Sikes. "If you'll walk over there and get into your car, Chief," she said calmly, "I'll take care of the problem."

I brought my own gun up slowly, careful not to lose eye contact with her. "Who do you think will win this standoff?" I asked her.

She hadn't expected an argument. I could tell because as soon as the script changed, she got edgy. Her eyes darted around like she was looking for a place to run to, and her hand started to shake. Trying to muster up her nerve, she said, "I'll kill you."

It was quiet and I almost had to read her lips, but I knew she meant it. Time to reason.

"Look, Diane. You get a slap on the wrist for stealing. Is it worth killing for? I don't think so."

Shaking her head now, she took a deep breath. "I've done it before. Killing Patrice wasn't easy, but I think I've got the hang of it now." Nervous little laugh.

I looked at the gun in her hand, then busted out laughing myself. "You killed Patrice with that?" I said.

It made her mad that I wasn't taking her seriously, I guess, because her grip on the gun got tighter and her eyes narrowed down to slits.

"That didn't kill Patrice," I went on. "Lady, all you did was shoot a corpse. I'm not even sure what the penalty is for that." I had an idea it was stiff, but at that moment my future health depended upon convincing Diane that she had never committed murder and that there was no need to start now.

She considered it for a while, then said, "You're lying. She was sitting in that car, staring at me. Challenging me."

"She was dead as a doornail. Her eyes may have been open, but I promise you, Patrice Gentry wasn't looking at you or anything else in this world."

I stood perfectly still, watching Diane and willing her to put down her gun. Maybe her hand dropped a quarter of an inch, but she was a steely woman, not about to give up without a hellacious fight. Speaking as softly as I could with all that pounding going on in my head, I went on. "Diane, I can show you the medical examiner's report. Patrice didn't die from a gunshot."

Nothing. She was like a computer, her mind whirring through the possibilities and options, undistracted by my argument.

"Why would you want to kill Patrice?" I asked. "I thought you liked the woman. *Every*body liked her."

At last! Her eyes welled up with tears and her voice broke when she said, "I thought the world of Patrice. I really did." She dared me to contradict her. "Killing her was the hardest thing I've ever done. But she was going to stop me. Like you, she was going to ruin my career, my life, everything."

"Patrice found out you were stealing from the nursing home?"

One nod of her head. "She took me aside Tuesday

night, said she'd noticed me slipping needles out of the supply closet. She wouldn't have thought anything about that, I'm sure. But there were PRN meds by some of the residents' beds."

"PRN?" I asked.

"Meds they're given whenever they need them. Given at my discretion. Nobody ever asks for them, though, so they sit there until they're out of date. They're wasted anyway. Patrice got the bright idea to check those and saw they were missing. She thought I was taking them. Personally taking them, like a user or something." She seemed offended by this assumption.

The new security light was shining right on her face, emphasizing angles that wouldn't have been noticeable in a softer light. She looked pale, like all the blood had been sucked out of her, and that made her seem like something more than human. Or something less.

"I see," I said. By this time she ought to have been weakening, but I couldn't spot any sign of it. That worried me. If she remained as tough as she'd been so far, I didn't think there was much chance of talking her down. And I'd been counting on doing that.

"Patrice wanted to get me into rehab." Diane gave a huff of snide laughter. "She wouldn't believe me when I told her I knew nothing about it. Just handed me that sweet, understanding smile and said all she wanted was to help me. The angel of mercy. She promised to keep quiet about it all if I'd get treatment, but otherwise she'd have to report me, *for my own good*."

"Did you tell her what was really happening?"

"What would have been the point in that? She still would have turned me in. I can't afford to lose my job. You don't know what I've gone through to get set up again since my divorce. I'm just now able to live comfortably. And life is getting better every day, I'll tell you. Jason owes me big time now, and he's found a way to raise more money."

I had a sinking feeling that Diane Forsythe would not be swayed by my assurances that she'd never be prosecuted for murder. She was caught up in her own web, guaranteed to lose her job now. Most people would kill to get out of work, but it was clear that Diane was willing to do the same to *keep* her job. Without it, she'd have no way of trading with Jason, and no way to keep and improve her lifestyle. Who knew? Maybe there was some prestige involved, a sense of identity for her. Maybe she found power in nursing. Whatever she got out of it, she wasn't going to give it up easily.

Back in the Sixties we talked a lot about the evils of materialism. Guess Diane missed that decade.

I stood there, gun pointed at her chest, wondering if I'd be fast enough to save myself. No way was I going to shoot first, but at point-blank range, there wasn't much chance I'd have time to shoot second.

"I could use a cigarette," I said. "How about you?"

She wanted one. I recognized the symptoms. That look on her face was just like the one on my own, reflecting a desperate craving for the feel of smoke scraping down the back of her throat. But she wasn't stupid, either.

"Get in your car," she repeated.

"Nope," I said. "Can't let you do that. I have to take you in." Talk about bravado!

"Get in your car. Now." She wiggled the gun in the direction of the parking lot.

We might still be standing there arguing about it if one of the night-shift aides hadn't chosen just that moment to slam open the back door and shout, "Diane!"

My nerves must have been half-shot, but Diane's were worse. She spun around and fumbled the gun. I didn't fully understand how seriously endangered I'd been until I heard the shot and realized it had ricocheted off the pavement. That little aide would have been dead if Diane had been calmer.

I was on top of her instantly, grabbing the gun and wrenching it out of her hand. Diane Forsythe fought like a tiger, scratching all the way.

In a burst of confusion, I looked up from my struggle with Diane and yelled to the aide, "Call the police." I don't know what I thought the lone dispatcher was going to do for me, but it didn't matter. The aide stood statuelike, her mouth hanging open in shock, making no effort whatsoever to call for help. Still, I can't fault her too much. That little lady saved my life.

By the time I'd gotten Diane's arms pinned behind her back, the other night-shift aide had joined her associate at the door and they were both watching us with fascinated stares.

"Sorry, gals," I said, when I finally had the situ-

ation under control. "I'm taking your boss to jail.
You'd better call the administrator and tell him to
find a replacement." I was gasping for breath and
trying not to show it. Embarrassed to be so out of
shape.

"But we need her," the first aide whined. "Mrs.
Steele is having one of her fits. That's why I came
out here—she's real bad, Diane. You've got to do
something."

Diane gave a jerk, but I held on tight. "I have to
see about her," she said to me, almost pleading.
"Mrs. Steele gets upset sometimes. She has bad
spells. I've got to give her something to calm her
down."

"You aren't the first person I'd think of when I
needed medical attention," I told her, feeling real
tough now that she didn't have a gun.

"She's right," the aide said. "Diane's the only one
who can calm her when she's like this. Mrs. Steele
needs her Valium and Diane's the only one who can
give it to her. We don't do shots."

The second aide nodded firmly, backing up her
coworker's claim.

Now, wasn't that a quandary? I couldn't very well
march the woman off to jail when she was the only
one of us qualified to care for that poor old lady in
the home. On the other hand, I wasn't crazy about
turning her loose inside the nursing home. Sometimes we just have to make a choice and hope for
the best.

"Okay," I said at last. "You can take care of this
one patient. I'll be right behind you every minute.
Meanwhile one of you girls"—I nodded at the

aides—"had better get on the phone and find yourself another head nurse."

The four of us marched down the hall of the
nursing home like drunken ducks, with me bringing up the rear. I'd made Diane take off her coat,
just to be sure she wasn't hiding anything else in
those big pockets. Meanwhile I'd tucked her gun
into my jacket pocket, where it kept threatening to
fall out, and I was still trying to figure out how to
keep her covered with my gun while not upsetting
any patients who might have been alert enough to
notice.

It was easy enough to find Mrs. Steele's room.
That would have been the one where all the noise
was coming from.

They had the poor old thing tied to her bed and
she was bucking like a bronco, trying to get loose
from the canvas straps. At the same time she was
wailing and keening and every now and then she'd
hit a note that positively blurred my vision. If this
was a regular event, I thought, I can't imagine why
Diane Forsythe would *want* to keep her job.

But I guess she was used to it, because Diane
went right up to Mrs. Steele and started smoothing
back the old girl's hair. She had one of the aides
bring her a disposable syringe, then she reached
into Mrs. Steele's bedside table and pulled out a little vial. She filled the needle, gave it a little thump
with her finger, and pulled back the bedcovers.
With one hand, Diane rolled the old lady onto her
side just enough to expose a wrinkled hip and
jabbed the needle in.

Seemed to me Mrs. Steele got still for just a min-

ute, long enough to let Diane jab her, before she
started thrashing around again. While we waited
for the drug to take effect, Diane held the old woman's hand and patted it with a slow, regular rhythm.

"Hush now," she whispered over and over. "Hush
now. I'm right here. Everything's okay."

Mrs. Steele kept hollering for a minute or two,
then slowly calmed down until she was able to talk
a little. "Diane?" she asked in a whiny little voice.

"Yes, ma'am," Diane said. "I'm right here."

"They're after me again," Mrs. Steele complained.

"Don't worry about it," Diane whispered. "I'll protect you."

Mrs. Steele gave a convulsive jerk, then calmed
right down. "You won't leave me, will you?"

"No, ma'am," Diane promised. "I'll be here for as
long as you need me."

It went on like that until Mrs. Steele fell asleep,
knocked out from a combination of expended energy and the drug Diane had given her. Even then,
Diane stood there holding her hand, adjusting her
covers, and whispering soothing promises.

"Time to go," I said, when I thought it was safe to
leave the old woman.

Diane looked up, resigned to her fate. She gently
placed the patient's hand under the cover and
turned to the two aides hovering at the door. "Keep
an eye on her. I'm sure she'll sleep through the
night, but keep a close watch in case."

Turning to me she said, "I have to chart the meds
I've given her."

"One stop to do that," I said. "Then we leave."

Diane nodded and slowly made her way around

the bed and out the door, with me on her heels. She didn't sit down at the desk, just pulled Mrs. Steele's chart and jotted a note in red ink about the old woman before putting it back in its place.

The two aides had followed us silently to the desk and now were standing there, not sure what they ought to do next. "Have you called for a replacement?" Diane asked.

One of the aides nodded. "Cathie Emory is coming in. She said she'd be here right away."

Diane didn't ask what Cathie had been told. She picked up her coat from where she'd tossed it on the desk as we came in and slipped it over her shoulders. "Okay, Chief," she said. "Let's do it."

All the way to the PD, with Diane sitting beside me stiff and quiet, I tried to match up the woman with the gun and the nurse who'd soothed the old lady's fears. It reminded me of that first time I'd seen Gentry, treating the little girl in the emergency room. On the surface, both he and Diane seemed like gentle, compassionate . . . well, angels. But underneath they were cold and hard and at least one of them was capable of murder.

Then I wondered which was the surface and which the real personality. Funny how we can never be sure about that.

CHAPTER

13

I pledge you my faith

AS SOON AS WE GOT TO THE STATION, DIANE insisted on calling her lawyer. I made that a priority, even handing her the phone and looking up the number myself. She got a promise he'd be right over to the PD, then she clammed up, probably on orders from the attorney, and sat like a stone on the cell cot.

Meanwhile I had to tell the tale of my evening's adventure to Bill, who listened with his mouth gaped open. "You mean a *nurse* pulled a gun on you?" he kept repeating. He didn't seem to care that Diane was locked up right behind us and could hear every word. He kept asking for details—more details than I could provide.

I also told him about Jason. Still no last name, but I figured we had a good lead now and it shouldn't take long to find out who that young man was, where he lived, and who his people were. Diane wasn't doing herself any favors by protecting him, and I knew her lawyer would realize that. Maybe we could wait a few hours and have her tell us everything, then I'd send German out to pick up Jason and there we'd be—case closed.

So. One mystery solved. I felt sure from the way she'd acted out in that parking lot—determined to take credit for killing Patrice—that if Diane had also cut the other woman's throat, she'd have insisted on telling me about it. And since she hadn't, it seemed I was still looking for a murderer.

But I had a lead on our burglar, small as it was, and I was feeling pretty good about my chances of catching up to him. Also I was looking forward to hearing his explanation. I know prescription drugs can be sold on the street, and needles, too. But antibiotics?

Having brought Bill up to speed, and ushered D. D. Maddox into the cell to confer with his client, I was on my way out the door when Bill got a call.

"It's the Med Center," he told me, hanging up the phone. "Teresa Simmons has just left the hospital with her husband and they thought you'd better take a look."

"What does that mean, she *left the hospital* with him? Did he hold her at gunpoint or what?"

Bill shrugged. "The nurse said Teresa left with her husband. Checked herself out against doctor's advice. Doesn't sound like there's a problem for us, but this nurse was worried about Teresa."

"Yeah. I am, too," I said. "I'll be at the Simmons house." I headed out the door, if not at a dead run then at a dead power walk. No telling what Ray Simmons was up to, but it sure sounded bad for Teresa.

I wouldn't have needed a patrol car's siren and flashing light for this one. In the middle of the night, Jesus Creek could be a ghost town. I knew

there wouldn't be any traffic to negotiate, and I
reasoned that if Simmons was in a rage, the noise
would only make him tighter. A calm, controlled
approach struck me as the way to go.

Sure enough, lights were on in the Simmons
house and both cars were in the driveway. I eased
up out front, parking my car so that it blocked the
drive and wondering if I'd have done better to leave
Simmons an escape route. I didn't want to go one-
on-one with him if he was drunk and mad. Or even
just mad.

Simmons himself answered the door when I
knocked. "Chief," he said, not making any effort to
welcome me. Take away one point for lack of hospi-
tality.

"Mr. Simmons, we got a call from the hospital. Is
the Missus here?" I tried to peek into the house,
but Simmons's mighty form was blocking the view.

"Yeah," he said.

"You know, Ray"—I used his first name like we
were good buddies—"she's in rough shape. The doctor wants her in the hospital for a few more days."

"Teresa's feeling fine now," Simmons insisted.
"She'll be a lot better off here at home. Where I can
take care of her," he added ominously.

"Well, Ray," I said, moving a little closer in hopes
he'd back up some, "why don't I talk to her and see
how she's doing?"

Simmons wasn't intimidated by me. He held his
ground and glared. "I told you she's doing fine. I've
got some time off from work and I'll be here with
her every minute. Whatever she needs, I'll see she's
got it."

"Ray, let him in." I heard Teresa's weak voice coming from somewhere in the room behind her husband.

Reluctantly Simmons stepped back and let me into the house. The living room was gloomy from the earth-tone carpet and furnishings. Even if the carpet hadn't been matted down from years of use, I'd have known it was an old one. These days carpets come in blue and rose, far as I can tell, and not many other colors.

A big plastic tree was stuck in one corner, collecting dust, and the only wall decoration that hadn't come from Wal-Mart was an eight-by-ten color photo of Teresa and Ray at their wedding. Even that was gloomy—Ray was wearing a brown suit.

Teresa Simmons was on the couch, bundled up in a ratty-looking afghan. Her bruises had turned yellow at the edges, making her look like she had some deadly disease. Without makeup and with her hair all flattened down and still showing some of the blood they hadn't yet been able to wash out, she wasn't half as attractive as usual.

I went over to the couch and knelt down beside her. "Miz Simmons, how you doing?" Simmons hovered over me the whole time.

She smiled at me, best she could, and pulled the cover up around her chin. "I'm feeling lots better, Chief. That's why I decided to come on home. Hospitals are creepy, and that food they give you—yuck."

Maybe she was trying to tell me something in code so Simmons wouldn't catch on, but damned if I could figure out what it was.

"The hospital said you checked yourself out, ma'am," I pointed out. "That might not be the best idea in the world. You've got serious injuries that need time to heal. And complications come up, you know. Sure you don't want me to run you back to the Med Center right now?"

Teresa looked up at her husband, then back at me. "Ray's going to be here with me," she said.

I stood up and tried to make myself as tall as I possibly could. Still looking her right in the eye, I said, "It's Ray that put you in this shape to begin with. You pressed charges, remember. He may not feel like being gentle with you after that."

"Oh, but he's sorry he did it," she said, pleading. "First thing tomorrow I'm going to call about getting those charges dropped."

"You can't just stop it," I pointed out. "The ball's started rolling now. The court's involved. At this point, your wishes won't carry much weight."

"You mean even if I don't want to go ahead with it?" She half raised herself up on one arm, indignant.

"That's right, ma'am. He's going to court on assault charges, first for knocking you around and then for swinging at my officer."

"Hey!" Simmons said. "What are you tryin' to do? She's *my* wife, damn it, and I've apologized. Teresa knows I'd never of hurt her if I hadn't been mad. We've got it straightened out now, so why don't you stay out of our business?"

Teresa was nodding her head, in full agreement. "He's right, Chief. This is personal and it doesn't concern anyone but us. I'm home, and Ray's here to take care of me. That's all there is to it."

I looked around the room, hoping for a clue that would make it all clear to me. There was that woman, bruised and broken, and she seemed to be convinced that her husband was a reformed man. I couldn't see any evidence that she was the least bit scared of him.

Didn't have any choice but to get out. Whether or not she could get the charges against him dropped would be up to someone else. I'd done my job. But if she thinks Ray Simmons will walk the straight and narrow from now on, she's got a surprise coming.

With a quick look over my shoulder in case Teresa wanted to change her mind at the last minute, I wished them a good evening and left. I noticed the garbage can had been set out by the road, ready for early-morning pickup, and there was a six-pack of Bud on top. I guess that was Ray's personal promise to his wife. I wondered if she'd thought that he could buy another one anytime he got ready.

I got back into my car and drove off, leaving the happy Simmons lovebirds to their reunion. Makes no sense, but most relationships don't. It all goes back to what I was saying before—couples spend their time thinking up ways to make each other miserable. Maybe Teresa Simmons liked playing that dangerous game. Maybe living with the threat her husband posed excited her in some sick way. Or maybe she wanted to believe he really meant it. *This time.*

* * *

The biggest problem with night shift is the rest
of the world is asleep and off duty.

I went back to the PD, where Bill was dozing in
his chair and Diane Forsythe had fallen asleep on
the cot. The only other human I could think of to
talk to was that nurse at the Med Center, so I
called her and reported on the Simmons family. We
talked a little bit about how foolish Teresa was being, and came to the conclusion that nobody can
help a woman till she wants to be helped. That
didn't make either one of us feel better.

A reasonably fresh pot of coffee was sitting in the
corner, so I helped myself to that and settled down
to ponder the mystery of Jason. I'd seen him twice,
but still hadn't gotten a good look at him. I was
tempted to wake Diane and try again to get information out of her, but I felt sure that would get me
slapped with harassment. Got to be careful about
how you treat criminals.

If I'd been on my toes, I'd have tried to jot down
the license number on that motorcycle when I'd
seen it in the parking lot, but at the time I'd had
Jason in my sights I'd been sure he was mine. Of
course, at that time I also thought there was nothing more going on in that parking lot than a mild
threat to Diane Forsythe. Guess that'll teach me
not to trust anybody.

Jason's helmet was propped up on the desk, and
I stared at it for five full minutes before admitting
that it wasn't gonna talk to me. That hour of the
night, all sorts of things seem possible. I wondered
if a psychic could have held that helmet in his

hands and picked up vibrations. Maybe a last name, DOB, or even general description.

Sometimes I have to laugh at my own foolishness. But I wasn't all that worried. Come daylight, I figured Diane would be ready to talk, or a little digging around town would lead me to Jason. Maybe the Johnsons would be more willing to help, if they *could* help.

I surely hoped that once I found Jason, he'd be willing to explain what the devil he was up to. Stealing VCRs and the like could be explained by his business with Diane. He probably got a tidy sum for the better items. What didn't make sense was why he'd spend that money, not on high-powered prescription drugs he could've used or sold, but on antibiotics and Band-Aids.

Another question: Why steal peanut butter and blankets? I didn't believe for a minute he could've hocked those for big money. Maybe Diane wasn't his only customer. Maybe he was trading the food and household items for—for what?

Hand it to Jesus Creek—we don't have run-of-the-mill criminals.

There didn't seem to be any reason to patrol the streets—I couldn't imagine that anything else would happen that night—but hanging around the PD, listening to Bill and Diane snore, didn't hold any attraction for me. At least in the car I could turn on the radio and listen to good music.

It worries me to hear my music called *oldies*. Some of those songs I can remember all the words to, just like they'd been on the jukebox yesterday.

Johnny Mathis; now, there's a singer. Why doesn't anyone sound like that these days?

Living in the past, I guess, is a big pretense. There must have been killers and wife beaters back then, too, but at least we didn't take it in stride. Crime wasn't the done thing, and when it happened, folks got upset about it. Not anymore. What's the last news story that really made you sit up and take notice? Hell, if the president came on the TV to announce we'd gone to war, most of us would just flip to another channel.

I got so het up about this that by the time I made my last check-in for the night, I was ready to jump down Bill's throat for letting the coffeepot burn. German was standing at the bathroom sink trying to scrub it out when I went in, and it teed me off so bad I just walked out and lit in to Bill.

"Sorry, Chief," he apologized. "I was asleep, I guess, and didn't notice. But look here—"

"Could you maybe not sleep on duty?" I wasn't in any mood to be rational, or fair. "Or turn off the pot first?"

"Yes, sir," Bill said. "But I've got to tell you something."

"What?" I snapped, halfway out the door.

"They've found James Barrow's car."

I stopped in my tracks and spun around. "Well, did they find Barrow to go with it?"

Bill was shaking his head. "No, sir. Just the car. It was parked beside a bridge. Barrow's shoes and his watch and wedding ring were on the front seat, and the keys were in the ignition. The car was all locked up tight."

"Did they find a note?" I asked.

"Yep." Bill was grinning. "It said he couldn't take the humiliation and that what he was doing was for the best."

Well, the whole story was so ridiculous I couldn't help laughing, which put me in a better mood. "I guess the rescue squad will have to drag the river. Too bad. I'm sure they've got better things to do today. How long you think it'll take?"

"Last time this happened, I believe it was about three days before they gave up."

I remembered it the same way. "Barrow's not too bright, though," I said. "He'll probably use his credit card right away and blow it wide open. Has anybody told his wife?"

"Beats me," Bill said, relieved that I wasn't mad at him anymore.

"Well, I'll drop by on my way home. She might have some idea where he's gone. And I'll bet she'd be glad to tell us."

German brought the coffeepot back in and started fresh coffee. He'd already heard the news about Barrow, and of course he'd seen Diane in the cell, so Bill had explained that to him. Al arrived for his shift just then, so Bill and I filled him in on the night's events, then I gave orders for the day.

"Find Scott Carter. Find Jason. And for Pete's sake, German, quit planning your wedding on company time."

His guilty look told me he'd been planning to spend the day on the phone to florists or tailors or caterers.

I went over to the cell, where Diane Forsythe

was sitting on the edge of her cot. She pretended not to pay attention to us, staring at the wall like she hadn't even noticed that we were in the room or that she was behind bars.

"Care to tell me Jason's last name?" I asked her.

Her only response was a wicked glance at me before going back to studying the wall.

"I want to know who Jason is," I said plainly. "German, if you don't get anything else accomplished today, I want you to find this kid."

"Sure thing, Chief," he said. "I'm having lunch with Pam and I'll ask her if she knows him."

"You're not having lunch, period, until I have Jason," I said, and left before he could argue.

I met Diane's lawyer as I was leaving the PD. Seems he'd scheduled a breakfast meeting with his client.

"Morning," I said to him.

"Chief," he said in response.

I never quite know what to do with this guy. Half the time he's hustling to defend some innocent falsely accused, the other half he's scraping up devious ways to get people like Diane off the hook. I've taken to being honest with him. I figure that's a concept bound to throw any lawyer off his pace.

"Diane's in big trouble," I told him plainly. "I sure wish she'd told me more about that boy—Jason. You might want to encourage her to be as helpful as she can."

Maddox grinned smugly. "Now, Chief. Diane is a victim. Lured into drug abuse, like so many people before her."

"What?" I said. "She told me last night she'd

never used drugs. Seemed to feel insulted that I'd
even think she'd do something like that."

Maddox shook his head in sympathy. "Poor
woman. She probably didn't know what she was
saying. I've discussed rehabilitation with her and
she is truly grateful for the opportunity to get herself straightened out and on the road to recovery."

I wasn't sure what was going on, but I knew he
was cooking up some clever defense for the woman
who'd tried to kill at least two people, me included.

"She wants to enter rehab?" I asked.

"Absolutely. And I feel sure her employer will
support her fully. It takes a brave woman to fight
her way back from addiction." If he'd been wearing
a hat, he'd have tipped it.

I wasn't sure how far sympathy would carry, but
I didn't doubt that the nursing home would fall for
it. If Diane claimed she was a drug addict and trying to break that addiction, she might be able to
keep her job. A jury probably wouldn't excuse her
attempt at homicide because of it, but it was only a
matter of time before Maddox remembered that Diane Forsythe had been acting out in response to
long-suppressed memories of childhood abuse.

I gave up all hope of seeing her serve time.

Anne Barrow was just stepping out her front
door on the way to work when I pulled up. She
looked at me like I was the devil himself, no doubt
expecting that I'd bring more trouble for her.

"I'm running late," she said, and started to go
ahead and get into her car. The kids were in the

backseat, and after glancing at me, Anne remembered to tell them to buckle their seat belts.

"I've got news about your husband," I said.

That stopped her in her tracks. She got back out and slammed the car door shut. "What's he done now?" she asked, eager like she wanted him to be in more trouble.

I told her about his car being found, not making any effort to break the news gently. When I'd finished, she busted out laughing.

"You think James killed himself to preserve his dignity?" she said, wiping tears from the corners of her eyes. "That would take guts, Chief. James is sadly lacking in guts."

I nodded. "Yes, ma'am. I thought it might be a fake. Mr. Barrow's wallet wasn't in the car. He'll probably have thought to withdraw enough cash to keep him going for a while. Can you tell me whether there's any money missing from your account?"

"From *my* account? James and I do not share our finances, Chief. He's totally incapable of managing money. I pay the bills and he gives me cash for his half of the expenses. He's just stupid enough to think he can get out of alimony and child support with this stunt."

I was relieved to see that she was taking the news of her husband's possible demise so well.

"Can you tell me, then, where he might go? He'll have to get himself set up somewhere. Does he have a friend who'd put him up for a while?"

Anne Barrow shook her head, laughing again. "James doesn't have friends. He's a boring, unimaginative man without the drive to succeed or the personality to impress. At this moment he is probably spending his last dime on a dingy hotel room within fifty miles of Jesus Creek."

"Well, ma'am," I said, "until we're sure, we have to assume he's actually killed himself. May I suggest that you at least call and cancel his credit cards? Wouldn't want some stranger to find those and go on a shopping spree."

She chuckled as if we'd shared a joke, and maybe we had. We both knew that Barrow would probably try to use the cards, and wouldn't he be surprised when he found out his credit had died before he had? "That would be just like James. To take off without cash at all, thinking he could live on plastic?" She broke out in a grin so malicious the devil himself would have envied it. "I'll cancel those cards right now, Chief. And I'll give you a call when I hear from James. I'm sure he'll be begging for help in a day or two."

She trotted into the house, happy as a clam now that she'd caught her husband in another stupid mistake. What a fine couple, I thought cynically. All the time at each other's throats, each one waiting for the other to make a mistake. And we wonder why the world's in the shape it's in, when you can't even walk the halls of your own home in safety.

Now, there's something to be said for the overeager rookie. Knowing German would, at best, make a halfhearted effort to locate Jason, I pulled up to Kay's house and got her out of bed. My intention was to tell her to work on the Jason case during her shift, but I knew she'd be too antsy to wait. I knew she'd be on it like hot butter on pancakes, *and* I knew she wouldn't quit until she found him.

"Looks like Scott Carter is off the hook for now," I told her. "Wherever he is."

"What makes you think so? Oh, did you catch our burglar?" She practically jumped up and down with excitement. "Sit down. I'll make coffee and you can tell me all about it."

As soon as I'd turned down her offer to make coffee, I filled her in on what had gone on at the nursing home the night before.

"Check with the Johnsons," I suggested. "I've told German to do what he can, but . . ." I spread my hands to imply that German didn't have the sense God gave a gnat.

Kay nodded her understanding. "Don't worry. I'll see the Johnsons first, then I'll hit the high school. Even if Jason is older than we think, he's probably not much older. Someone there will at least be able to give me a list of all the Jasons they've had in school in the last few years."

"Just our luck to get the most popular boy's name of the decade," I said. "Whatever happened to naming boys after their fathers? I don't believe I've ever met a grown man named Jason."

"So what? You'd have named your kid *Reb*?" she said.

"That's not my real name," I pointed out. "I was named after my father, being the first boy and all. That's how it ought to be."

Kay sneered at my fine sense of tradition, but

he didn't say anything about it. "Are you sure Ja-
on and Scott aren't working together?" she asked.

"You've got it in for Scott, haven't you? What's
he deal?"

Kay just shrugged and tapped her finger on the
able. "I think it's odd that Scott would disappear
t the same time the break-ins started. With his
istory, he's a perfect candidate. In any case, he's
nissing and we ought to be looking for him."

"Fine," I agreed. "No problem. We're looking for
he boy. Odds are, if we find Jason and if Scott's in-
olved in the burglaries, Jason will tell us every-
hing we need to know to charge Scott. Best way to
ake some heat off himself."

Kay nodded. "Did you try to get information
bout Jason from Diane? Did you promise her it
vould help her defense?"

"No," I said. "Why would I promise her that? Let
er lawyer figure out how to help her defense. She
ried to *kill* me."

"I'm sure it was nothing personal," Kay said, and
grinned. "Lots of us want to kill you from time to
ime. It's not like Jason can help her, after all.
She's bound to lose her job, and heaven only knows
vhat other trouble she might be in. I'd think she'd
e more than willing to help us all she can."

"Diane Forsythe is a stubborn woman," I pointed
ut. "Or is that redundant?"

CHAPTER

14

Constant fidelity

GETTING TO SLEEP THAT MORNING WAS NO problem at all. I collapsed on my bed and had just enough time to remember that exactly one week before, I'd been dragged out to the nursing home to investigate the death of Patrice Gentry before I fell sound asleep. My last waking thought was that I'd killed a week and had nothing to show for it in the way of progress.

By the time I woke up, the shadows had moved across the room and I gauged it to be around six o'clock or so. I stretched real good and rolled over onto my back, relaxed as I'd ever been. With hours to go before my shift and nothing pressing to interrupt, I decided to stay right there and enjoy being lazy.

Naturally, though, I couldn't stop myself from thinking about what all had gone on in the days past. Anne Barrow and those kids of hers came to mind. It surprises me whenever a mother turns out like that. You'd think instinct would tell her to take care of her young'uns, but I guess that's only the case with animals.

She sure got feisty when it looked like the kids

were going to be taken away from her, though. Maybe she'd learned something from Patrice Gentry, after all.

On the other hand, if a mother will kill to protect her children, maybe Anne Barrow had killed Patrice to protect her motherly rights. Anne *said* she was grateful to Patrice for pointing out the error of her ways, but Patrice wasn't around to tell us any different.

It occurred to me that Anne Barrow might also have killed her husband, for any number of reasons. Sure wouldn't be the first time a husband left his dirty socks on the floor one time too many. And Anne wasn't even making a pretense of being upset by James Barrow's sudden disappearance. I felt sure she was smart enough to make it look like a suicide, too. Even smart enough to make it look like Barrow had *faked* his own suicide.

Good police procedure demanded that I maintain a vigilant search for the missing and/or late Mr. Barrow. Most likely he'd tried to dodge the troubles he'd brought on himself by running away. He hadn't been smart enough to think through his actions before. Remember, he'd never even considered that he might be convicted? If that was a pattern for him, and I had no reason to think it wasn't, he probably hadn't thought out how to disappear.

That's not as easy as you'd think in this day and age. We're all numbered. Barrow couldn't get a job without his Social Security number. Chances were, he'd learned, like the rest of us, to depend on a credit card. If not, he'd almost surely have made a large withdrawal from his account before he left. I knew Anne Barrow wouldn't mind letting us take a look. If she was half as smart as the average bear, she'd have made a large withdrawal from his account—assuming she'd killed him. It would make us more inclined to believe that he'd run off, and it would also give her some extra spending money for those long nights on the riverboat.

I made a mental note to keep a close eye on that woman. For one thing, if she'd done away with her husband, she was bound to slip up sooner or later. For another, I didn't trust her as far as I could throw her with those kids. It seemed like a good idea to enlist Mrs. Weldon for a little unofficial surveillance, too.

On top of that, I thought I'd better check up on Dr. Gentry, the man himself. There'd been so much going on I hadn't had time to call that hospital in Houston to see if he'd even gotten there. Wouldn't have surprised me a bit if he'd taken off for parts unknown, and that would be embarrassing as hell. After all, I'd given him permission to go.

Maybe Amanda was in touch with him, I thought. For that matter, she might have taken off with Gentry. I could picture the two of them living it up on a sunny beach somewhere, although I supposed Gentry would be tanning while Amanda saved the beached whales.

And I still didn't have a motive for Gentry to kill his wife. He had enough money, although some people just can't *get* enough. If he was one of those, and if he'd thought he was going to profit from his wife's estate, he'd be a mighty depressed man right now.

Having a wife hadn't interfered with his social life one bit, that was for sure! I've known of men killing their wives for freedom, but Gentry seemed to have way more of that than he needed.

And alibis? The man had a million of 'em. So here was a perfectly good suspect with no motive and, as far as I could detect, no opportunity.

I kept fishing for possible motives for Gentry while I showered and dressed, coming up empty. That didn't satisfy me, though, because sometimes the motive is so darned silly that nobody but the killer understands it. Like that guy who killed his wife because she ate the potato chips. Guess it made perfect sense to him at the time.

By the time I drove into town, it was already dark and the houses along Morning Glory were lit up from the inside. A few people were still working in their yards and I could smell the sweet scent of fresh-cut grass. Daffodils were already starting to fade, but that didn't matter to me because I knew it was a sign that spring was rolling right on into summer—that much closer to your homecoming.

I passed Kay on the square and motioned to her to turn around and follow me to Eloise's. I'd done so much thinking about the Gentry case that it had knotted itself up in my head. I couldn't have sorted it out alone if I'd tried all night.

"You look chipper," Kay said, getting out of her car and slamming the door. "Sleep good?"

"Finally," I told her. "You had anything to eat lately?"

"As a matter of fact, I was feeling the urge for roast beef and potatoes with gravy," she said.

"You've got impeccable timing. I almost ran into Jason tonight."

I raised an eyebrow, waiting for her to explain.

"He came traipsing out of a house, backpack bulging with stolen goods, and crossed the street right in front of me. Didn't recognize the unmarked car." She grinned, taken with the idea that our run of bad luck with transportation had proved an asset this time. "Hopped on his motorbike and cruised away, with me right behind him."

"Tell me he's locked up and I'll kiss you."

I didn't like the way she frowned. "Sorry, Reb. When I tried to pull him over, he took off like a shot. Up the hill and right through the woods, not far from the city limits. My car doesn't do off-road racing."

Kay wasn't to blame for that. I couldn't even blame Mayor McCullough, since it would have taken at least another motorcycle to follow Jason through the woods. I wasn't even sure that would have worked. "You did good," I said to her. "We'll check for tracks, see if we can figure out where he goes."

I held the door open and we went into Eloise's and took a table in the corner. Henry Mooten and his outlaw gang were huddled together at the center table, earnestly discussing something that I was sure I didn't want to be let in on. A few locals were scattered around the room, but none of them seemed to be breaking any laws, so I relaxed and enjoyed the moment.

"Are you hearing anything about Henry's campaign?" I asked Kay.

She nodded happily. "He's got a lot of support. You know McCullough is off on another one of his 'business trips.' "

"Where to this time?" I asked. "Jamaica? France?"

"Myrtle Beach," she said. "Guess he doesn't want to go too far from home with a competitor nipping at his heels. Patrick hasn't been the most devoted mayor we've ever had. But you know, I don't think he's bright enough to notice how much trouble he's in."

"Would *you* worry about a rival who's mapped out the city, looking for the most likely place for the aliens to land? Besides that, McCullough's never worried much in his life. Certainly not about jobs. He probably doesn't care whether he wins or not," I pointed out.

Kay nodded agreement. "I wish a real candidate would enter the race. Lacking an intelligent, well-informed choice, I suppose I'll vote for Henry. How about you?"

I looked out the window at the two personal cars Kay and I had arrived in. I calculated the odds of getting even one patrol car repaired in the near future. And I glanced over at Henry, who might not be operating on full standard time, but who at least cared enough to mount a campaign as opposed to Patrick's show-up-on-election-day strategy, and made my decision. "Yep," I said. "I reckon I'll vote for Henry."

Eloise came over with coffee for Kay and me and made herself comfortable in the extra chair. "Me, too," she said. "Henry might not do so bad."

"Heard any more about his campaign promises?" I asked her.

"Well, I know you'll be glad to hear he's talking about reliable transportation for the police," she said, ticking off the items of interest. "And he's talked about a community pride program. Something like Sunday afternoon rallies in the park, where we'd all be encouraged to present programs of our own choosing. I thought the women's choir from the Baptist church could put on a gospel show one day."

I rolled my eyes. Not that the women's choir doesn't have talent, mind, but those bright pink choir robes they wear could blind half the population on a sunny day.

"Never mind," I said. "It'll be easier to vote for him if I don't know what's in store. Kay was talking about roast beef and that sounds good to me. Pile me up a plate, Eloise."

Kay told her to make it two plates, and Eloise scooted off to the kitchen to pass the word on to the cook.

"I wonder if German and Pam have thought about having their wedding in the park," Kay said. Sounded a little dreamy, like it wasn't German's wedding she was picturing. Poor old Wayne.

"Why don't you suggest that to him?" I said. "But for the life of me, after all we've seen of marriages this past week, I don't know why the man doesn't make a run for it now."

"What do you mean?" Kay asked, indignant. "The Barrows? Well, Reb, all marriages aren't like that."

"Damned close," I pointed out. "It's just occurred

to me that Anne Barrow may have killed her husband and that's why he's up and disappeared."

"Not a chance," Kay said. "He's a wimp. He couldn't face the trouble he's gotten himself into and he took off. I'm sure Anne is glad he's gone, too."

"I reckon most people would be glad to get rid of their spouses. And a gracious plenty of 'em have killed for it. Besides, any woman who'd go off and leave her kids like Anne Barrow did wouldn't think twice about killing a man, would she?"

Kay didn't have an answer for that one, so she moved on. "I talked to Mrs. Weldon today. She's fuming about those kids going back home."

"Yeah, I knew she would be. Thought I'd ask her to keep an eye on that family and let us know if anything looks odd."

"I wish we knew," Kay went on, "where James Barrow is. We've assumed he went off and left the kids alone. Maybe there's more to it. Could be he's in bigger trouble than we know."

"If not now, he will be. I don't guess you've heard any more about him today." Kay shook her head no. "Then I believe I'll stop by and talk to Anne again this evening. See if she's heard from him."

"Don't you think she'd call us first thing? Nothing would make her happier than to have him hauled off to jail."

I didn't doubt that for a minute. I could imagine Anne Barrow standing outside the PD, grinning and gloating, while we booked her husband.

"You know Teresa Simmons is back home?" I

asked, and watched her eyebrows shoot up. "She's forgiven the big lug."

"Touching," Kay said snidely. "Next time she calls us to come rescue her, I'll try not to hurry. Maybe they'll make up before I get there."

I could understand her frustration, but I thought I'd better remind her of her sworn duty to protect and serve. "Lawsuit," I said simply. She got the point.

"How about Jason?" I asked. "Any word from the Johnsons?"

Kay pulled a notepad from her front pocket. "The Johnsons say they've had three Jasons who participated in the dances and Bible studies, none of them regular. Also none of them have been around lately. The school records show an uncommonly high number of Jasons and they're all within the same age range. This is going to be harder than I thought."

"Well, did the Johnsons happen to remember one Jason who rode a silver motorcycle?"

Kay shook her head. "They said the kids sometimes arrive together, in one car or another. Sometimes two of them on a motorcycle. Some even ride bikes, and a few walk. Neither of the Johnsons pays much attention to vehicles. I asked them to let us know if any of the Jasons shows up again. They said they would, but—"

"But? But what?"

Kay shrugged. "They seemed hesitant. My guess is that they want to talk to this Jason before we do. They may have some idea of convincing him to turn himself in."

Great, I thought. Do-gooders will get you every time. "Let's keep an eye on the Johnsons' house, then. Watch for that motorcycle."

The food at Eloise's just keeps on getting better and that roast beef was an award winner. I felt so good by the time I'd polished it off, I almost didn't mind when Henry Mooten came over to our table.

"Chief," he said, "Kay. Good to see both of you out. I've heard about all the work you folks have been doing lately."

"Trying, Henry. Trying," I said with a weary grin. "We're all worked about half to death."

Henry nodded thoughtfully. "I've been discussing that very problem with my staff," he said. Dead serious. "Now, I'm not promising anything at this point in time, but I may have a solution to the shortage-of-manpower problem."

I was surprised when Kay let that word *man-power* slide. She must have been serious about voting for Henry.

"Anything at all you can do, Henry," I said sincerely, "would be appreciated. If it was up to me, I'd shoot you right into office this minute, just on the strength of effort."

Henry stuck his hands in his pants pockets and looked modest. "Well, now. It ain't definite. We've got to work on this plan a bit more, but I don't see why it wouldn't work. Good talking to you."

He was back at his own table before I could get the details of his plan, but I didn't much care what they were, so long as they got me some extra officers on the street.

It was full dark by the time I left Eloise's, promising to meet Kay back there for ten o'clock coffee. I drove around behind the PD and filled my gas tank from the city pump, then took a few minutes to clean all that stray trash out of the car. Funny how driving around in my own car doesn't feel like work. It feels like I'm lost out there in the big bad world with nowhere to be.

Didn't see any point in cruising the rest of Kay's shift for her, so I went back to the house and turned on the television to kill a few hours. There's not much worth watching these days and I couldn't even find an old movie anywhere. Maybe it's time I subscribed to one of those channels that can be counted on to show Hollywood classics twenty-four hours a day.

I put it on some brainless sitcom and even tried turning off the color, but it still didn't hold my attention. Next thing you know, my mind had wandered back to the Gentry case and the confusing possibilities.

Maybe Jason was our killer, after all. If he'd been in the habit of lurking around the nursing-home parking lot while he waited for Diane to take her smoke break, he might have had words with Patrice Gentry. Diane had made every effort to kill Patrice in order to protect her job and the measly bucks she got out of Jason. Who knew what *he* was up to? But it might seem just as important to him as Diane's job seemed to her.

I had a feeling the Johnsons could have delivered Jason to us on a platter if they'd been so inclined. Maybe if I nudged them, wore them down, they'd decide he wasn't worth protecting. It struck me that I'd been negligent in not keeping a closer eye on what goes on out at that place. Anytime you've got kids congregating, you gotta ask why.

The presence of a gruff but lovable old cop might prevent unfortunate incidents in the future, too. Yep, I decided I'd definitely talk to the Johnsons and offer my services as counselor and guardian. Sooner or later, one way or another, I'd get Jason.

I'd keep busy watching out for the Barrow kids, too, I figured. There were two good reasons for that—protecting the tots and keeping an eye on Anne Barrow. For the life of me, I couldn't find anything in my experience to explain her behavior, or her husband's. Nothing except what I've seen so many times before—husband and wife going at each other with any weapon they can find. For the Barrows, the weapon seemed to be emotional rather than physical. They took great joy in terrorizing each other, like a couple of bullies playing chicken.

You can't help but wonder what the kids will be like. Sometimes I think people ought to be screened before they're allowed to reproduce, although so far I haven't thought of a way it could be done without becoming big business for a handful of government bigwigs. Maybe I should put Henry Mooten to work on this.

No doubt I'd feel compelled to watch over Teresa Simmons, too, even if she'd brought most of her troubles on herself. Surely the woman knew that sleeping with Gentry was going to get her knocked

around. Had she honestly thought Ray wouldn't
find out about it?

I wondered if Gentry's sudden departure for
Texas had been prompted by his fear of Ray Simmons. Would've been enough to send me running.
And who knew how many other husbands were just
now discovering what Gentry had been doing with
their wives? But then, Gentry had said he'd been
angling for that job for a long time. And all the
while his wife had thought they were going to
Somalia to save the world.

So far there'd been not a hint of improper behavior on the part of Patrice, but I still had my suspi-
cions about her and James Barrow. In fact, if
Patrice hadn't been so obviously dead, I'd have expected to find her and Barrow traveling the highway of love together. Couldn't say I'd blame him for
leaving his wife for Patrice Gentry.

But lacking a jealous wife, I couldn't think of
anyone who'd had it in for Patrice. Except Diane
Forsythe, and she was already nabbed. It still
seemed like the best suspect in the case was Steven
Gentry, and the man had so many alibis it made
me dizzy.

Sometimes you just have to word it in the right
way before you make the connection. That's what
happened to me right then. Steve Gentry's alibis.
What's wrong with this picture? I asked myself,
and pondered it for a minute before the answer
shot into my head.

Gentry had enough alibis for three or four people.
My second-best suspect was Teresa Simmons and
either she *and* Gentry were lying, or she had a

good alibi, too. But if Teresa Simmons was telling the truth, then Amanda Brewer didn't have an alibi at all.

CHAPTER

15

Together in holy bedlock

I LIT OUT OF THERE LIKE A CAT WITH ITS tail on fire, praying I'd come up with a motive before I got to Amanda Brewer's house. That's an indication of just how frustrated I was—the woman didn't have an alibi and I was ready to convict her. I had to force myself to slow the car to a reasonable speed while I got my heart rate down.

Her car was in the driveway and there were lights on all over her house. I couldn't see any sign that she had company. Making my way to the door, I thought about what I'd say to the woman. You can't just go riding in, accusing someone of murder, after all.

The door was open to let the fresh night air blow through the screen. Amanda met me wearing jeans and a man's shirt. Not fancy enough to be one of Gentry's, I noted. Her hair was pulled back with an elastic band and there wasn't a lick of makeup on her face. Well, at least I knew Gentry wasn't going to walk in on us or she'd have herself fixed up for him.

"Evening, Miss Brewer," I said cordially. "Could I come in and talk to you a few minutes?"

"Well, sure," she said, pleasant as could be. She
seemed mighty pleased about life in general. "Excuse the mess," she added as I stepped inside.

And there was plenty to excuse. Clothes and
books and I don't know what all were scattered
around the living room. She had to sweep an arm-
load of jeans off a chair before I could sit down.

In one corner of the room was a partially packed
suitcase. "Taking a trip?" I asked her.

She nodded her head like an eager kid. "I'm join-
ing Steve," she said jubilantly.

Well, well. So Gentry wasn't going to set up
housekeeping alone in Houston.

"This must have come up all of a sudden," I said.

Amanda kept folding clothes and placing them in
organized stacks on the couch—jeans, T-shirts,
socks, so forth. "I've spent all day closing up the office. Haven't quite finished yet, but I should be
ready to go by the time he gets back from Texas."

Funny. Gentry hadn't sounded to me like he was
planning to return to Jesus Creek anytime soon.
"I'd expected the doctor to be tied up at his new job
for a while yet," I said.

"I'd think we'll be there a year or more," Amanda
said. "Whew! Everything is happening so fast." She
stopped fiddling with the clothes and perched on
the arm of the couch. "I deserve a break. Would you
like a drink, Chief? Or a snack?"

"Coffee, if you've got it ready. That sounds good."

She hopped right up, full of energy, and said, "I'll
be right back."

Right back is a fuzzy term. I sat there staring at
the walls for a couple of minutes while listening to

215 Deborah Adams

her make kitchen noises. Pure boredom drove me
to cast a glance at the suitcase. Neat packer, our
Miss Brewer. A place for everything, it seemed. But
everything wasn't much. For the most part she was
taking jeans, old shirts—casual wear. I hear they
don't dress up much in Texas, or maybe she was
putting all her nice clothes in another suitcase.

On the table beside me she'd stacked her bank-
book, birth certificate—the important papers you'd
want to carry with you, instead of putting them
into a suitcase and chance having the airline lose
them forever. Not that I'm nosy or anything, but I
felt an overwhelming urge to see how much money
she had in that passbook. You wouldn't think a
nurse would have an impressive salary, so I was
surprised that she had a savings account at all.

Imagine my surprise when the passbook turned
out to be a passport. Brand-new, it seemed. Did
Texas declare independence?

As soon as I heard her heading for the living
room, I dropped all those papers back on the table
and assumed an innocent pose.

"Coffee's perking," she said. "I've got cheese and
crackers, some fruit, and a few cookies. We may as
well eat it all, since I'll be throwing out the food before I leave."

"This has all been sudden, hasn't it?" I asked.

She nodded again. "It certainly has! I got into the
office yesterday and found a message on the machine from Steve. He said he'd had to go out of
town for a few days and that I should close up the
office and pack because he wanted me to join him."

"I must have misunderstood what he said to me,

then," I admitted. "Or maybe I don't know how it's done. I was under the impression that Dr. Gentry would be on staff at some hospital. But you're saying he'll still have an office and you'll be the nurse, is that right?"

Amanda fairly giggled. "Chief, I think you *have* missed something. Steve will be running a clinic, just like he always has before. Somalia probably doesn't have a decent hospital."

"Somalia?" That put me back a few inches. "Gentry told me he'd given up on that. Said he couldn't handle it without his wife by his side. What happened to the job in Texas?"

Now it was Amanda's turn to be confused. "A job in Texas? Oh, no, Chief. Steve is going to Somalia just like he'd planned. I'll be taking Patrice's place."

She stood and motioned for me to follow her into the kitchen, talking all the while. "It's a wonderful opportunity to help the people there. I'm honored that Steve has asked me to go along."

I pulled out a kitchen chair, still too stunned to sit in it. "Now hold on," I said. "Dr. Gentry is all of a sudden giving up this great new job in Houston to go to Somalia?"

"What job is that?" she asked, not overly concerned. She'd pulled out a couple of apples and started slicing them to go with the other snacks.

"The one he couldn't wait to get to," I said. "The one that pays big money and showers him with prestige."

She stopped chopping apple long enough to look

over her shoulder at me. "What on earth are you talking about?" she asked.

"Look, the man came to me and said he had this job offer, that he'd been trying for a long time to get this job, and that he had to leave right away. I remember he said something about having you close up the office here, but I had no idea you'd be going to Texas. In fact, I had the distinct impression that he was looking forward to a clean start down there."

It shook her. "Well, that's just not true," she said, either amused by my ignorance or aggravated by my thickness. "Somalia has been on his schedule for almost six months. The only reason he hasn't already left is because he was waiting for Patrice to wrap up her affairs here."

Rusty gears started to turn. I knew that Patrice had been talking to folks about that Somalia project and that she'd been eager to get started. I also knew that Steve Gentry didn't have a passport to his name, and if he was enthusiastic about helping the poor souls in a war-torn land, he'd managed to conceal it from me.

"So you've spoken to Gentry?" I asked. "Recently?"

"I told you, he left a message. It was very clear. He said that he was leaving for a while and that he wanted me to close up the office and then to replace Patrice." Then, as if I'd questioned her statement, she added, "He said he'd made the arrangements for me to go along."

We could have been speaking two different languages for all the sense it made. What sort of game was Gentry playing? I wondered. And why would he have bothered to lie about taking Amanda with him, whichever place he was going? It wasn't like he had a sterling reputation to protect.

Amanda had chopped up a half-dozen apple slices by the time I figured it out. "Miss Brewer," I said, "have you been living in the firm belief that Dr. Gentry is on a mercy mission to the world?"

She spun around, recognizing a slur against her idol when she heard one. "What does *that* mean?" she demanded.

"Steve Gentry never had any intention of going to Somalia," I said. "Else why would he have applied for this job in Texas? And why wouldn't he have gotten his passport renewed? Did you know it's out of date?"

She glared at me. "He was waiting for Patrice. She kept coming up with excuses not to go. Apparently"—a little sneer here—"she enjoyed the cushy life here too much to worry about death and disease in another country."

The cushy life in Jesus Creek? I looked at that big old knife in her hand and another gear creaked.

"You thought Patrice was keeping him from his God-appointed mission, didn't you? I suppose he told you that one. And I can understand how you'd believe him. But did you ever talk to Patrice about it?"

She didn't say a word, just stood there looking like she didn't know what to think, but definitely leaning toward Gentry's version.

"You killed her, didn't you? You thought if you did away with Patrice, Gentry would marry you and take you on his world travels."

Amanda raised the knife and pointed it at me. "Some things are bigger than a single human being. Patrice was a wonderful woman once. When she first told me about all the places they'd been, the conditions they'd suffered through, I thought she was an angel. But then she changed. Poor Steve was so eager to get back out there, to *do*. Patching up scraped knees is a job for a worn-out old man. Steve has so much more than that to give."

I was fully aware of the weapon she held, but not overly concerned. After all, there was a table between us and I had a gun. No contest.

"Maybe we ought to talk this through," I said calmly. "Here's the facts, little lady. Steve Gentry never had any intention of going to Somalia. Call the hospital in Houston where he's now on staff. Ask them how long he's been trying to get that job."

She wasn't impressed, so I went on. "Patrice Gentry had a passport ready to go. Weeks ago. She's been telling all her friends how much she was looking forward to it. I doubt Gentry's ever brought the subject up himself."

I could see her flipping through her memory, trying to recall exactly what Gentry had said about Somalia. The defiant set of her shoulders told me I'd hit pay dirt, but that she wasn't ready to give in yet.

"Oh, and there's something on that tape you didn't hear quite right. What Gentry told me was that he'd arranged for you to replace Patrice *at the nursing home*. He wanted you to have a job when he left. You didn't actually hear him say he wanted you to come along to Somalia, did you?"

Again, I could tell she was replaying that message. And I knew I'd found the correct translation. Too bad she hadn't.

"So," I went on, "you decided that if Patrice wasn't in there, gluing up the works, then Gentry would ride off to save the world. And I suppose you thought he'd marry you. Make you the only woman in his life?"

Her head jerked back like I'd punched her. I decided to rub in a little salt. "How could you be sure he wouldn't take Teresa Simmons? Or one of the others? You got any idea how *many* women that man's sleeping with?"

"Steve is a unique man—" she started.

"Where were you the night Patrice Gentry was killed? The night Gentry was sleeping with Teresa?"

I had my hand on my gun, easing it out of the holster just in case I needed it. It was impossible to tell what she was going to do. I doubt Amanda knew.

"Miss Brewer, I'm gonna have to take you in. You have the right—"

That's as far as I got. She slammed the knife into the hardwood surface of the kitchen table, then jerked it out again in a fit of rage like I ain't never seen. I whipped my gun up and pointed it right at her. "Don't make matters worse," I advised. "You're under arrest."

I thought for sure she'd drop the knife, but I was wrong. On the bright side, she didn't attack me. Instead, she held the blade against her throat and grinned at me.

"You can't save me with a gun in your hand," she said. "And if you put it down, I'll kill you. One of us is dead."

Personally I hoped it would be her, but that isn't the official position. I had to stop her from hurting herself, and I thought I could probably do it even without a gun. But I wanted to think through my options first, and I wasn't sure I had time.

She'd already punctured her throat with the tip of the blade. I could see a bright red drop forming on her skin. So concerned about saving the world herself, Amanda naturally assumed that I would sacrifice my own life to save hers. Unfortunately, I felt a slight compulsion to do just that. A handicap that sometimes accompanies the badge.

The sound of the gun nearly deafened me and besides that, it scared the hell out of me. I was absolutely certain I hadn't fired.

Amanda was slammed back against the counter and the knife went spinning through the air, finally landing in a corner of the kitchen floor.

"Hold it right there," I heard a gruff but definitely female voice say.

I jerked my head around just long enough to catch a glimpse of Kay coming through the kitchen door, gun held out in front of her like a big-time TV cop. Meanwhile Amanda's arm had started bleeding like all get-out, and she was shaking like a leaf.

I tucked my gun back in its holster, grabbed a dishtowel, and wrapped it around Amanda's wrist. She didn't put up a fight. Amanda may have been idealistic to the point of insanity, but even she had to know when it was over.

* * *

"That's twice in a week that a woman has saved my life," I said, thinking back to that night at the nursing home when the little aide barged through the door. "It's bad for my self-image."

"Get over it, Reb," Kay said. Stuttered, rather. It was almost two hours later and she hadn't calmed down yet. We'd been so busy getting Amanda patched up at the Med Center, then booking her and filling out reports and calling a lawyer for her, that I hadn't had time to talk to Kay about what had happened.

"How did you know I needed help?" I asked. "More of that intuition you're always bragging about?"

"N-not exactly," she said. "I spotted your car and wanted to let you know we've found James Barrow. He was arrested in Arkansas. Got into a barroom brawl. When they ran him through the computer, they discovered that he was supposed to be dead."

"When his wife finds out, he'll wish he was," I said.

"I was going to tell you at shift change—didn't want to wake you since you never get enough sleep as it is. But then I saw your car at Amanda's. I started to knock on the door and I heard what was happening in there. Scared the life out of me. At that point, my intuition told me you needed help."

"Well, I'm right proud of the fact," I admitted. "And that was an impressive shot. Took the knife right out of her hand."

"I was aiming for her leg," Kay admitted. "I'd

never aim that close to the upper body unless I really meant it."

I wondered what she'd have hit if she'd been trying to kill. Me, probably. Now, Sarah, honey, don't take this the wrong way. But you women are dangerous, you know that?

Let no man put asunder

FROM *THE BENTON HARBOR SUN*:

SATTERFIELD AND HUNT ARE MARRIED

Pamela Jacqueline Satterfield and German Donald Hunt were wed August 28, 1993, at the VFW hall in Jesus Creek.

Theirs was a double-ring ceremony in Western motif. The Reverend Richard Wagoner of Jesus Creek Baptist Church performed the ceremony in front of an authentic hitching post.

The bride wore a midcalf, lightweight denim skirt and a white cotton blouse with lace inserts. Her accessories were a denim, lace, and silver ribbon hairpiece, bone-leather Western boots, Western hip belt made of bone leather with silver conchos, and a blue bandanna hand-tied with beads. She carried a bouquet of bluebonnets and baby's breath.

The groom wore a Western beige suit, Stetson hat, snakeskin boots, and a bolo tie.

The bride was attended by matron of honor Sarah Elizabeth Leach. The groom was attended by best man Robert Lee "Reb" Gassler.

At a reception immediately following, the Western motif was continued, with blue bandanna material covering the bride's and groom's tables. Centerpieces were baskets of bluebonnets, yellow mums, and small potted cacti.

The bride's cake had two metal horseshoes and yellow mums as part of the cake decoration, and the groom's cake was decorated with a Western boot. San Antonio punch was served.

Taped music was played throughout, including selections by Tish Hinojosa, George Jones, Skeeter Davis, Jim Glaser, and Randy VanWarmer, with the bridal march being "Mama, He's Crazy," by the Judds.

The bride and groom are making their home in Jesus Creek, following a honeymoon in Texas.

A good time was had by all.

In Jesus Creek, Tennessee, murder seems to be ALL THE rage....

ALL THE GREAT PRETENDERS
ALL THE CRAZY WINTERS
ALL THE DARK DISGUISES
ALL THE HUNGRY MOTHERS
ALL THE DEADLY BELOVED
ALL THE BLOOD RELATIONS

**THE JESUS CREEK MYSTERIES
by Deborah Adams**

"Ms. Adams's books perfectly capture the rhythms of life in a small town, where everyone sees it as a God-given right to know everyone else's business."
—*The Baltimore Sun*

The award-winning
Jesus Creek mysteries
by
DEBORAH ADAMS

---◦---

**Published by Ballantine Books.
Available in your local bookstore.**